Petticoat Marshal

Gunfighter Cort Packet rides into the town of Scarlet intending to kill Yucca Frazel, but many try to prevent him: Frazel's employer rancher Addison Blackwell, an Indian agent cheating Apaches out of goods, a gunfighter rumoured to have murdered the marshal's husband, and the marshal herself – Rebecca Rogers, trying to find the truth about her husband's death, forced into being marshal in a fixed election by the powerful rancher who professes warm feelings for her. But are the feelings for her, or are they for the riches on her land?

Before Cort can finish his business with Yucca Frazel, he finds himself caught up in killings, treachery, stealing and politics that threaten to leave him lying dead.

Petticoat Marshal

George Snyder

A Black Horse Western

ROBERT HALE

© George Snyder 2019
First published in Great Britain 2019

ISBN 978-0-7198-2939-0

The Crowood Press
The Stable Block
Crowood Lane
Ramsbury
Marlborough
Wiltshire SN8 2HR

www.bhwesterns.com

Robert Hale is an imprint
of The Crowood Press

The right of George Snyder to be identified as
author of this work has been asserted by him
in accordance with the Copyright, Designs and
Patents Act 1988

Typeset by
Derek Doyle & Associates, Shaw Heath
Printed and bound in Great Britain by
4Bind Ltd, Stevenage, SG1 2XT

ONE

Cort Packet woke sweating with the nightmare. He jerked to his elbows and wiped his face, waiting for images to fade. Physically, he was aware of two things: the pain along his left shin from Yankee cannon-fire balls twelve years before and Amanda's auburn hair sprawled over his chest.

The image faded, but remained.

1865, a forgotten field during a forgotten battle, somewhere in Georgia. They stretched in line twenty feet apart, each manned by eight soldiers, firing low with steel balls. Cort had no feeling in his left leg from the ball that shattered it; he knew he might lose it. He crawled toward one of the cannons. The two Remington pistols he found were empty. He found an old Remington .44 with two shots fired. His Colt Navy .36 was loaded full. Through smoke and field mist he fired the Remington, killing four men. Two others ran. Still on his belly, Cort dropped the Remington and drew his Colt. The remaining two Yankee soldiers stood by the fuse ready to fire again. He shot one in the stomach, the other in the side. He used the cannon wheel to rise and shot them in the face. When they fell, he stumbled along the hot cannon barrel and looked down at two boys, ready to fire again. One might have been sixteen. The other was no more than thirteen or fourteen. As Cort watched, the youngest jerked and vomited over his face, the puke coming up with blood. Cort cried out in anguish. The war ended for him on that day.

Amanda moved her face to his and kissed him on the jaw. She showed a frown of concern.

He fell back while his breathing returned to normal.

'The nightmare?' Amanda asked. She moved closer to hug him.

He felt pain in his left leg. 'Careful,' he whispered.

She raised to look down at his face. 'The leg giving you bother again?'

'Usual early morning. It'll pass once I'm up moving around.'

Her lips moved to his. 'I'll be gentle with you.'

He kissed her well and caressed curves under the flannel gown. He grimaced when she moved her long leg over his. 'Easy.'

'You'd better find time for us, mister,' she said.

He smiled at her. 'You'll know it when I do.'

She turned and slid up with her back against the head-board. She placed her hand on his chest. 'I hear rustling behind the curtain. The wild child will soon be among us. You better finish Billy-Boy's room soon.'

The cabin was one room built of logs with a cold room basement. Furnishings were a table and four chairs, a counter with sink and wood stove, curtains hiding their double bed and across the room another curtain for Billy-Boy.

'I figure one more month,' Cort said. 'The boy grew faster than we thought. I shoulda started the room years ago, but there were fences and stock and furniture building the last seven years. Who thought he'd shoot up like a weed?' He beamed at her. 'I like that, the way you do that.'

'What?'

'Whenever you talk to me, you got to be touching me someplace. We sit at the table, you place your hand on my arm. When we're standing, you wrap your arm around my

6

waist. Even with others around, it don't matter. If I'm in a chair, when you come up to talk you sit on my lap. Just want you to know I like it. It pulls you closer to me.'

Amanda's green-eyed gaze softened. She looked at him long enough for her eyes to become shiny. 'How do you do that, Cortland Packet? How, after eight years of marriage do you still find ways to tug even more love for you from my heart? Not only words. You still pull a chair out for me. When you hunt, you come back with a fistful of flowers. You keep doing it, making me love you more than I ever thought I could love a man.'

Cort smiled. 'A fella does what he can.'

'You'd better find time for us today. I mean it, mister.'

'Mebbe you already tamed me some.'

'Hah! I doubt that.'

He heard the boy dressing behind the curtain across the cabin. 'You made me want to give up the life I had, the life of the gun.'

She studied his face, her auburn hair tousled, high cheeks rosy, lips full. 'Do you miss it, Cort? The excitement, the action, the moving around?'

There had been those times for him, but less in the past few years. 'Life with you is better and keeps improving.'

She moved her face close to his. 'And why did you choose me over Martha?'

'A couple of Irish lasses fresh off the stagecoach. You was younger and a lot better looking. I liked the way you filled your dress.'

She acted shocked. 'You're shameless.'

'Still do in fact.'

She pressed her soft lips to his and moved against him for a lingering minute. She quickly turned her head away. 'Mercy, mister, I do believe I'm getting stirred up.'

The pound of child feet raced across the cabin from

behind the boy's curtain. Billy-Boy bounded to the bed and leaped on his pa. 'Hey! Time to get up. We got work to do.' He wiggled between them as Cort tousled the boy's curly brown locks.

Amanda pushed her face close to the boy's. 'Somebody has a birthday tomorrow. Could it be the wild child?'

'No, it's *me*. I'll be seven.'

'I need an assistant baking the birthday cake.'

'But I got to help Pa on my room.' He turned from Amanda to Cort. 'Can I have a gold coin for my birthday?'

'What gold coin?'

'From when you sell steers. The metal box buried in the basement.'

'We'll see.'

'Pa, I seen her through my window jest at dawn. That one-eye Butter busted the stall gate open again, went wandering off.'

Cort swung his legs to sit on the side of the bed. 'I better get after her before she meanders too far.'

Amanda said, 'She likes them yellow flowers down in Buffalo Canyon. You want me to hold breakfast?'

Cort nodded to Billy-Boy. 'This one needs his milk. If she's in the canyon it'll take a couple hours. She'll be easy to spot with that butter shade and full udder, though she can't see too good.'

'Take me with you, Pa.'

Amanda pulled the boy to her. 'You got arithmetic first. Milk and biscuits and arithmetic before your pa gets back.'

'Aw, Ma.' Billy-Boy looked from one parent to the other. 'When do I get my baby sister? You said I was getting a baby sister.'

As Cort dressed in his tan canvas pants with copper rivets at pocket corners, his blue calico shirt, deerskin vest, and boots, he and Amanda looked at each other with smiles.

Amanda said, 'Your pa and me are working on that.' She gave Cort a smoky look. 'Aren't we, Pa?'

'Yes'm,' Cort said. 'A fella does what he can.'

Cort rode away from the cabin. Whiskey, the six-year-old chestnut was still frisky and had given him a couple bucks before he settled. Cort carried the Peacemaker and kept the cane next to his Winchester scabbard on the Texas saddle. He only needed the cane in the early morning when he first rose and when it rained, but sometimes it was needed if he climbed chasing some steer. He had practised mounting the saddle every day after it happened until he could do it without much pain.

The Union army had a practice of filling a gunpowder can with half-inch and one-inch steel balls. When the cannon was loaded and ready to fire, a fuse was lit on the powder can and it was shoved down the barrel. The aim was low, intended to kill and mutilate. The cannon fired seconds before the gunpowder fuse went off. The powder exploded and steel balls scattered to tear off limbs and rip out intestines as they flew. Cort had caught a half-inch ball across his left shin, hard enough to shatter the bone beyond complete repair.

No need to ponder on it. The nightmare kept coming back, but he had come off much better than other men who lost parts of themselves. It was war. Twelve years ago. He was twenty-four, older than the boys around him, and had been a gunfighter and bounty hunter since age eighteen after his half-Cherokee ma had died.

Cort followed the track of Butter, the milk-cow, until he figured to hear the bell. The trail led southwest from his sixty acres – that he had won playing poker in Tombstone. Billy-Boy would spread hay for the twenty longhorns and heifers, then take care of the livestock. He was a good boy, though Cort thought he must get lonely being so isolated. Cort tried to take his family to Santa Fe at least twice a year. And there were the neighbors. Amanda's sister Martha had married a miner named Ned Perry and they owned a small spread of fifteen acres two hours away. No children for Billy-Boy to companion. Other neighbors with children were closer, but high toward Raton Pass and longer to reach.

He liked the life with Amanda. She was what made the living of it good. Being isolated like they were, no gunmen came around looking for a reputation. Cort still practised, an act that did not sit well with Amanda. She had told him more than once that Billy-Boy would not live by the gun.

Since Butter the one-eyed milk cow had been wandering since dawn, Cort did not figure on finding her much before noon, if not after. While he saw signs of her trail, he mostly headed for Buffalo Canyon with the flowers she liked.

Amanda had grown with her sister in Ireland then London where their ma worked as a lady's maid in a big mansion. The growing girls did cleaning chores without pay. Their pa had worked the railroad and was killed by a falling rail. The ma naturally assumed Amanda and Martha would also be lady's maids. After their ma died, Amanda at age seventeen had the gumption to break away, and dragged her sister, who was four years older, aboard a clipper bound for Boston. They worked as maids in Boston while Amanda taught herself to cook and sew and read and write. She stood in front of a mirror for hours watching her mouth, talking American English to rid herself of the Irish lilt. Now and then a bit of brogue still slipped out. From the beginning she told Martha she would marry a man of the west, and in the west, she would settle.

One night in Tucson Amanda was accosted by four

gunmen who liked the cut of her dress and the fall of her hair and decided to help themselves to beauty and sister both. It turned out Cort was after the *hombres* who were on Wanted posters for bank robbery and murder. He was still a bounty hunter at the time and cut all four down in front of the two women. Though shocked at the brutality, Amanda fixed her Irish green eyes on twenty-eight-year-old Cort Packet, and he had no chance.

Beyond the mesa ahead were three more mesas that stretched to Buffalo Canyon. April sun brought warmth, but not enough to eliminate the frosty bite. Cort wore his buffalo coat. He kept his straight black quarter-Cherokee hair no longer than his neck, and his flat-brimmed plains hat was brown and worn. Though he listened hard, he only heard the clop of Whiskey's hoofs over rocks and earth as they walked along. No need to run along this ground. Too many rabbit and prairie dog holes waited to break a horse's leg. And too many hoof-splitting rocks.

Along about noon, a covey of quail scattered to the sky far ahead, almost out of sight among aspen and juniper. Cort stopped. He squinted forward, a bluff to his left, a flat-topped mesa in front, Buffalo Canyon behind that. He still did not hear the clang of the cowbell. From in front, a rabbit scurried past him and behind, running fast.

Cort unhooked the rawhide thong holding the hammer of his Colt Peacemaker .45.

TWO

Once beyond the mesa, Cort Packet heard the cowbell of his one-eyed milk cow, Butter. Buffalo Canyon dug through high sandstone cliffs with a stream gurgling down the middle of prairie grass. Side to side, it stretched no more than a hundred yards or so. Different shades of flowers clumped on the cliffs and bunched in places along the stream – purple, yellow, orange, shades of red. Spring weather kept mesquite bright green and would for a couple more months. Butter stood with her front hoofs in the stream chewing her cud. She looked up as Cort entered the canyon. The bell clanged softly.

Beyond Butter, a Mescalero brave sat his pinto pony watching Cort approach. He looked not much past twenty, dressed heavily in deerskin with a buffalo hide coat. His lean face was unpainted.

'I see you, Cort Packet.'

'I see you, Lorenzo Wolf Eater. Did you come to steal my milk cow?'

'I do not know if it is your milk cow. It stands alone eating flowers. How do I know it belongs to you?'

Cort nodded to Butter. 'She has my mark on her rump, Circle-P, from my barn.'

'Circle-P might mean many things. Any man might burn

Circle-P into a milk cow rump.'

'There is writing inside the cowbell that tells her name is Butter and she belongs to me.'

Cort looked around for signs of others. He reached for his lariat, ready to drop the loop over Butter's neck.

Lorenzo Wolf Eater said, 'The children on the reservation go hungry. Five died in the winter.'

'You know my place to the north?'

'Yes.'

'Come by this afternoon. We will give you two gourds of milk for your children.'

'We need more than milk.'

'The government gives you beef, and blankets to keep you warm.'

'The blankets are tattered. The beef is rotten in places and crawls with maggots and worms and flies. The government agent steals from us.'

'Then stop him.'

'We will. When summer comes and he does not listen, we will stop him. He has been warned, but like all white faces the words of warning go through him without stopping.'

Cort had the loop around Butter's neck. She paid little attention to him. 'I gave you beef last winter.'

Lorenzo Wolf Eater crossed his hands in front of him and nodded. 'Fine beef. The roasted taste was good and it satisfied the belly. But you have more beef, more than enough for two people and the small one, Billy Boy.'

'Some to eat, some to sell, some to breed.'

'We do not have so many. A man should not have so much when those around him are starving.'

The two men stared at each other while Butter continued to chomp flowers and chew. Cort wondered if the brave thought one half-blind milk cow was worth the

13

exchange of lead. But it was more than a cow. If Lorenzo Wolf Eater was lucky and killed Cort, the way to the small ranch and all in it was open for him and his braves – steers, pigs, chickens, goats, rabbits, garden vegetables – and the woman. Billy Boy might be taken to raise or killed on the spot.

Cort knew the sleazy way Government Indian Agents handled those on reservations. In his past he had collected the bounty on the worst of them, rarely taking them in alive. The Government passed laws, but the execution of those laws was left to mousy little clerks and the worst slime walking. It was plainly shown to him when those of the South suffered the results of the Reconstruction. Originally from the Pecos of Texas, he witnessed his state join the Union after it had been a Republic, then break with the Union when hostilities broke out. He had fought for Texas, not any southern cause, and lost.

He now saw what Government did to the original natives, using snake-oil peddlers called Indian Agents. Could be that some agents were honorable men, actually doing good for those forced to live on reservations – just not any he had ever met.

While Cort watched the brave closely, he was reminded that the nearest he came to connection with authority was collecting bounty money from the local sheriff. And that was all the connection he ever wanted. Now he owned a small spread that gave him a decent living and a woman and boy worth loving. That was all the reconstruction he needed. The best thing any force in power could do was just leave him alone. The best thing Lorenzo Wolf Eater and his people could do was to take from the agent everything due them. And if the agent resisted? Make it look accidental.

Pulling to tighten the lariat holding Butter, Cort said,

'When you come by this afternoon I will give you a steer. I cannot give you a cow because I only have four, plus this one-eyed milker. I need the cows for breeding.'

Lorenzo Wolf Eater sighed deep. 'Cort Packet, you are a good man. But we are more in number than you. We cannot settle for just one steer.'

'Then there will be trouble between us.'

'If trouble comes, you will lose everything.'

'And you will lose many braves.'

'But we will take your steers anyway, all of them. You have too much. We have nothing.'

Cort moved Whiskey so the chestnut stood sideways to the brave. He drew his Colt and aimed. 'We can settle this right here.'

Lorenzo Wolf Eater sat tall and stiff. He looked beyond Cort, behind him with his eyes wide. 'Cort Packet, look.'

Cort was ready to drop the brave out of the saddle. 'Nothing for me to see.'

'Smoke,' Lorenzo Wolf Eater said. 'It rises far to the north. I see it. Look!'

Cort spun the chestnut around. The column of smoke rose thinly from far off. 'That's near my cabin,' he shouted. He heeled Whiskey hard as he dropped the lariat and holstered the Colt. The chestnut leaped forward at a full gallop.

THREE

One hundred yards from the burning cabin, Cort Packet filled his hand with the Colt once again. Heeling Whiskey, wishing the chestnut would run faster, his thoughts filled with betrayal. What if Butter had been taken from the stall by Lorenzo Bear Eater and taken to Buffalo Canyon to lure Cort away from the cabin? Mescalero braves might then raid the small ranch and take what they wanted, including the woman.

His attention moved fifty yards ahead as he searched for Amanda and Billy-Boy. He saw white men, not any braves. Four of them, three riding out of the yard, whooping and hollering, one with Amanda's jewelry box, another with the silverware drawer. The fourth held a torch, and was riding from the burning cabin to the barn. The barn was still intact, not burning. The rider's arm went back to toss the torch.

There were three horses in the barn.

Without hesitation, at thirty yards, Cort shot the man in the chest. He stayed in the saddle until Cort's second shot hit the side of his head. His Montana Peak hat flew off and he followed, leaning to the side and dropped to the ground. The torch fell next to him. Cort rode into the yard and turned Whiskey toward where the other three had gone.

16

'Amanda!' he shouted. 'Billy-Boy!' He heard nothing except the crack of burning wood as the cabin began to collapse and retreating hoofbeats. He felt the heat of the fire, smelled the burning pine. He looked down at the man, but did not know him. He rode after the others.

A rider came fast from Cort's right. With the hammer of the Colt cocked, he aimed.

'Cort!' Ned Perry cried. 'Don't shoot. It's me.'

Cort continued at a slower pace as his brother-in-law came alongside. 'I picked up the fixed busted axle of your wagon in Santa Fe. Thought to bring it later in our wagon. I seen three of them, Cort, headed that way.'

'Amanda?'

'No sign. Mebbe in the house.'

Cort heeled Whiskey. They came to the stream and crossed it. The body of Billy-Boy lay under a juniper along the bank, half of his curly brown head bashed in. The skull looked broken in half.

'Ah,' Cort cried. 'Ah, no.' The sense of loss dominated rage. The boy's little hand was balled into a fist. 'No,' Cort said again. His eyes stung. His throat tightened to where he could not swallow. He swung down from the saddle in leg pain and limped to the body. He knelt and placed his hand on the boy's chest. 'Ah, my Billy-Boy, no.' Pain creased his heart. He fought to swallow.

'Cort, look over there,' Ned said. He still sat in the saddle.

One of Amanda's sandals lay twenty feet from the body of Billy-Boy. Cort heard limbs crack as a man ran toward them.

'Cort,' Ned cried, then pulled his Remington when the man came around a willow and fired. The shot split a willow branch. The man fired at Ned. The shot hit Ned in the leg. His sorrel reared and Ned fell out of the saddle and smashed against a juniper. He slid down with his face against the rough bark.

Cort drew and shot the man twice, belly and head. The crack of the shots echoed through the valley. Before Cort went to Ned, he picked up Amanda's sandal. He looked around the area. He went to the man and used the toe of his boot to turn him over. He didn't recognize him. Now Cort feared the worst for Amanda. With a lifetime of seeing and causing death, he knew she was gone.

Ned tried to push to his feet.

'Can you ride?' Cort asked.

Ned coughed and threw up against the juniper. He jerked and retched with his head against the tree. 'I can't ride.' He looked down at the leg wound. 'It looks bad, Cort. I think the bone is shattered.'

'Your face is scratched up some too.'

'Yup, except that was – Cort, we got to get them other two. You got to ride them down. Look what they done to Billy-Boy.'

'And likely Amanda. Sit tight until I catch them. I'll be back.' He mounted Whiskey and rode out in the direction the men had taken.

A quarter mile out from the ranch, he saw Amanda's tattered green dress.

One hundred feet farther, he saw her.

She lay in a soft small meadow, her body naked and blood-covered. She had been ravaged and beaten. Her sightless green eyes looked half-closed, her lovely face wrinkled in pain. The bruises and blood on her legs showed it might have been all four. They attacked her and Billy-Boy before they set the fire. She had fought them, and that probably got her killed.

Cort used his thumb and index finger to close her eyes. He sat next to the body, rocking back and forth, his eyes closed. He faintly heard the gurgle of a stream. A gagging gargle sound came from his throat when he tried to say her name. Tears filled his eyes and eased down his cheeks, blurring his vision to where he could not see her clearly. His chest continued to empty of soft feeling, emptiness that had started with the sight of Billy-Boy. Her ended life had taken any such warmth and love with her. Already he felt icy coldness waft through him like a forest fog that refused to release the trees. He held her hand against his chest. She had all of him for eight years. Even after he knew nothing tender could touch him because he led a hard life of the hunt and the gun and killing, she managed to crawl in his heart and touch him with her sensitive delicate ways. He had learned that even he was capable of loving and of being loved. No more. Rage began to replace grief.

Two more were left. If he could, he would make sure their death came long and slow.

Cort ignored the pain in his leg. He wrapped the body in the tattered green dress and picked her up. She felt light in his arms and still held the scent of light perfume, of orange juice and warm bread spread with churned butter and apricot jam. He gently draped her over his saddle. He would sit behind and hold her on. Whiskey could handle the weight.

When he got back to Ned, there was a torn shirt sleeve wrapped around the wounded leg.

Ned nodded to the stream. 'I didn't know what to do with the boy. Mebbe they intended to take the bodies to the barn before it burned too bad.'

'I'll make two trips. If you can't sit a horse, you'll have to drape yourself over the saddle.'

'I can't. My leg is on fire. Well, you know. You went through it in the war when your leg got blown apart.'

Cort studied his brother-in-law. They had never been

close. Ned was a small man, small in stature, small in think-ing, small in action. Cort never really liked the man. He tolerated him because he was married to Martha, Amanda's sister. The rumor had been that Ned Perry stole silver ore from the mine he worked so he could buy the small spread close to the Packets. Martha had wanted that.

'All right,' Cort said. 'I'll come back for you. For now, I'll be taking your sorrel.'

Cort tied the small body of Billy-Boy over the saddle of the sorrel and without a backward look rode to the small ranch.

The cabin was now a smoldering skeleton. He gently placed the bodies in the barn and returned to Ned.

'I'm bleeding bad, Cort.'

'Can you put your foot in the stirrup?'

'I can't move. I'm about to pass out with the pain.'

'Mebbe you ought to do that.' With his shoulder pushed under Ned's belly, Cort lifted the small man to drape him across the saddle. Ned remained quiet on the ride to the barn.

When the bodies were stretched and covered, and Ned sat leaning against a post, Cort said, 'You didn't bring the axle to fix the wagon. I'll ride to your place and bring Martha and your wagon back. Be gone about four hours. You rest easy.'

'You got anything to eat?'

'You need rest.'

'I been through a lot, Cort. I know, you lost your whole family, but I'm hurting here getting my leg shot up helping you plug down them jaspers.' His voice squeaked as he talked faster. 'And now you leave me with bodies. I emptied my belly throwing up. I need something to eat, some sub-stance to keep me alive.'

'Sure, you do, Ned. We all need something. All I got was

burned. I'll get Martha to bring food.'

'That will take a long time.'

'No matter how long it takes, I intend to make sure everybody gets what they deserve.'

FOUR

The two graves were dug on a grassy mound, Cort's own hands on the shovel. He built the simple pine caskets. For words on the wooden headstones, he inscribed the names and dates and the word 'beloved' for each – 'beloved wife and mother' for Amanda, 'beloved son' for Billy-Boy. He dressed the bodies the best he could from what Martha brought. All the clothes of Amanda and Billy-Boy had been lost in the fire. He nailed the coffins shut.

Each act hardened him more.

The only attendees for the burial were Cort, Martha and Ned Perry.

Cort said words about rest between the eternities, words he had heard once. He finished by saying, 'They belonged to me and were taken from me. They are already there, already in whatever special place the good and loving go. I carry their memory and will live with that.' He put on his hat and walked away.

In the barn, where Cort had built a small table, Martha spread fruits and vegetables and smoked ham. She was small like Ned, only spindly without much in curves. She wore a stark tight black dress from ankle to throat. Her pinched face looked ten years older than Amanda's, not four. She had never had a child and had tried hard, without complete success, to hide her jealousy of Amanda. When Cort met the sisters, during his draw and fire on those four outlaws, Martha was much more shocked than Amanda. The men had accosted the sisters and threatened more. Now looking at her, Cort reckoned she had grown knowing she was not as pretty as Amanda and drew less attention from men. Even those four wanted outlaws from years before went after Amanda, maybe following up with the not-quite-lovely sister. Jealousy was there. She had warned her younger sister to stay away from the gunman. He was trouble and would leave her in a sleazy hotel room destitute and puffed with child. Yet, through their eight years together he liked to think it was the younger sister who lived a happy life. A devoted husband, a bouncing baby boy, a small successful ranch, a house filled with love and laughter. And Martha showed she was shocked at the way the couple carried on with each other, acting like newlyweds after five years, even after eight years. Jealousy. Martha revealed it now in her small pinched face with her dark grey-streaked hair in a tight bun. Jealousy for Amanda and hate for him.

Cort sat with a small plate of smoked ham and sliced tomatoes on his knees. The tomatoes came from Amanda's garden. Ned, with his wrapped leg and crutches, sat to the right. Ned sweated in the barn and appeared uncomfortable. Maybe he was not a man for burials. Martha sat in front facing Cort. She had ham on her plate but did not eat. Her thin lips worked in and out as she stared at him.

'I told her not to pair with you, Cort.'

Cort said, 'And many other things about me, most not true.'

'You're a killer, a gunfighter having no business with a sweet, loving, devoted woman. You should have stayed with those whores, those soiled doves from the saloons you lived in.'

Ned cleared his throat. 'Come on, Martha. Maybe it started like that. But eight years. He's nothing like that now.'

Martha spun her head toward him. 'You shut your mouth. I seen the way you looked at her. Every time we visited, you never moved your eyes away, always tried to get close.'

'Now, you're just being silly.'

'What makes you think he won't just go back to his killing ways?'

Cort said, 'There are two left.'

Ned nodded and blinked at Cort. 'Then what? You reckon to come on back here and start up again?'

Martha turned back to Cort. 'Bring one of your saloon snippets to take Amanda's place?'

'Just shut up, Martha,' Cort said.

'Hey,' Ned said. 'Easy on that kind of talk.'

'Then you tell her to shut up.' He turned to Martha. 'I'm done with this kind of life. It only worked with Amanda. You take the steers and livestock and I'll sign over the deed to Ned here. Do what you want with the place. Sell it, rebuild and move on it, I don't care.' He pointed a finger at her. 'Don't mess with them graves. I may come by to visit them from time to time. I don't want them ever disturbed.'

Ned rubbed his wrapped leg. 'You got that, Cort. That's generous of you, brother. Ain't that generous, Martha?'

Martha said nothing, just stared at Cort with her pinched face.

Cort didn't care for Ned calling him brother. He didn't like Martha much either. He wanted done with them, done with this place. He had other places to be, other things to do. A man chose his friends; relatives came without choice.

To Martha, he said, 'It ain't like I snatched Amanda from a nunnery and had my way with her. I was a gunfighter bounty hunter. That had been my life since eighteen, during and after the war. Mebbe it will be again, I don't know. The girl marched into me with everything she was and I had no defense. It wasn't nothing a gun could handle. She took me over and I belonged to her. It ain't never happened before and it won't happen again.'

'Humph,' Martha said. 'So, you say. Amanda isn't here to say otherwise.'

Cort sat straight. 'Mebbe I want you to get some idea that there's a chance I made the girl happy. She did smile and laugh a lot.'

'You convince me of nothing. I can't even think of you two together. You must have physically hurt her something awful, forced yourself on her with your big hands, made her submit to unspeakable acts.'

Ned frowned. 'Martha? Martha.'

Martha clamped her lips tight and looked away.

Cort stood. 'With that, you folks can leave. Mebbe you can get back to your place before dark.'

They stood. Martha said, 'I always thought Amanda was some kind of slave to you.'

Cort stepped to the barn door opening. 'Martha, I don't give a damn what you think. Take your buggy on out of here.'

Ned picked up his crutches and hobbled beside Martha to the wagon, both of them the same height. He looked up to the graves on the small hill then turned back to Cort. He looked in pain. 'Will you swing by our place before you leave?'

'I doubt it,' Cort said. 'You come and help yourself to the stock. I'll mail you the deed.'

Everything personal he owned had been destroyed in the fire. No need for a pack horse. Time was wasting. The next day he sifted through the basement ashes and dug up the tin box from two feet down. In it were the property deed and gold coins from the sale of steers over the years, enough to keep him going for a spell. One coin was to be for Billy-Boy's birthday.

Just before noon, Cort cut out three steers and herded them to the nearby reservation for Lorenzo Wolf Eater and his people. They were grateful, and sympathetic over his loss.

The rest of the day was spent in the barn doing the paperwork to transfer the property to Ned Perry. It would be in Ned's name as the man, but Martha would control everything. He made sure the stock had plenty of feed. In a day or two, the animals would be collected.

He slept in the barn with the chestnut Whiskey and the three other horses. Before he drifted off, he thought of hateful words shot at him by Martha. Mostly, he thought of what she had said about Ned and his longing for Amanda. It was understandable all men would have looked on Amanda with lust and longing. The sight of her beauty brought out primitive thoughts. Cort accepted that as the way of men, and how the sight of his lovely wife affected them. He never minded men looking, or even longing, as long as it never went further.

He slept little, and in the morning packed and having eaten leftover ham, he rode to the hill to say his final goodbye to his family. He stood over the graves with his brown plains hat against his belly. 'Amanda girl, Billy-Boy, I may not be back this way ever again. I may never be the man you once knew. But I want to thank you, girl. Thank

26

you for our beautiful son. He would have grown straight and clean with much more of you in him than me. Billy-Boy, you look after your ma now. Wherever you're headed, she'll need you.' He sighed deeply. 'Thank you, Amanda, for your deep love. Thank you for the eight years you made me a better man, so much better than I could be without you. You had every good part of me. I ain't never going to be there again.'

Cort turned away from the graves. He put on his hat and looked to the west, out toward the Rio Grande with Santa Fe beyond. The two men had headed in that direction. They had left behind the crushed boy, the ravished woman beaten to death, and the burning cabin, and Ned Perry with a shot-up leg. They had taken what treasure they could carry and rode out, rode west. That was where he would find them.

FIVE

Utah Bill Slaughter waited outside the ranch house for the others to leave. Inside, listening to ranch owner Addison Blackwell, were the ranch foreman Red Jack Wheat and Yucca Frazel. Yucca rode in two days before from the east around Santa Fe, rode in with a shot left hand to see his trail pard, Jesse Ryan. Had quite a story to tell as Utah recalled, about setting a cabin afire and some gunslinger coming after him. Utah stood outside in the dark and smoked a store-bought cigarillo. He reckoned New Mexico Territory might be getting too thick with gunslingers, himself included. Some of the fastest were in Arizona Territory, down around Tucson and Tombstone, or up around Abilene and Cheyenne. The men inside stirred for the door.

Red Jack Wheat took the lead coming out and stretched his hand toward Utah. 'Yucca, you never met Utah Bill Slaughter. Utah, meet Yucca. You probably seen him come in.'

Yucca squinted at Utah. Neither man offered a hand of friendship. 'You got the smell of gunman, Slaughter. I heard about you from when me and Jesse rode trail. From around Abilene. Heard you got no conscience about shooting a man in the back.'

'Neither did Hickock,' Utah said.

Yucca stepped forward. 'Heard last year you dry gulched our marshal there in Scarlet.'

Utah touched the rawhide holding down the hammer of his Colt. He did not lift it off, just touched it. 'The marshal drew down on me. It was a fair fight.'

'Heard that. Only it was late at night. The way the wounds angled it might have been three guns like mebbe you had some help, a couple of boys in the shadows.'

Now Utah did flip the rawhide off his Colt hammer. 'You making an accusation?'

Red Jack Wheat stepped between the two men. 'We got enough going on around here without in-fighting. Yucca, you go on out to the bunkhouse. Jesse is there. You got one more day of easy living with that hand. Day after tomorrow I want you and Jesse moving Longhorns.'

The booming voice of Addison Blackwell came from inside the ranch. 'Slaughter, get yourself in here. You fellas can jaw-jab in the bunkhouse.'

Utah re-hooked the Colt rawhide as he stepped inside by the front door. His spurs jangled when he walked, though he did not work cattle, but just liked the sound. He fingered his pencil mustache. His dress, all in black with silver trim, gave him the image he wanted. Working cattle was not part of it. His job was ranch security, which meant many things to different men. He did remove his hat when he entered the den.

The rooms inside the ranch smelled of men without women. There were Mexican maids to do necessary but unimportant chores, but no mistress ruled with a feminine hand. Utah reckoned his boss, Addison Blackwell intended for the widowed female marshal, Rebecca Rogers, to eventually take over those duties. That was only one reason Utah had been brought to the ranch. To remove the

29

husband Alfred Rogers as marshal. That way, in an election by merchants that Addison controlled, the wife would be the new marshal. She had been deputy, and she handled a double-barrel twelve gauge well enough. Besides, though Scarlet was not exactly a sleepy town, not much on the surface really happened. There were rumors of silver ore about. And the Indian agent Newt Dugan lived much richer than an Indian agent should. Gossip had it the Triangle-B owner's wild nineteen-year-old son Dougie was sparking with Libby Dugan, doing a lot more than kissing and feeling. To Utah, it was all usual small-town stuff. With him coming to town, the population had gone up to 1,500, then dropped by one. And now it looked like it might drop a couple more.

Utah sat opposite the desk from Addison Blackwell. A box of fine cigars was on the desk. Blackwell did not offer them. Utah had worked for men like Blackwell before. He wore a tan business suit, looked distinguished for a man in his fifties, and had become slightly bent in stature due to worry. Owning the biggest ranch in the valley, he worried over the drop in beef prices and the future of his town, Scarlet. It took a while for Utah to figure the name of the town. Then one day he saw it for himself. When the sun set, the buildings and surrounding area turned a bright red, a scarlet that touched everything outside. Blackwell had not built the town, he just owned it.

Addison Blackwell said, 'I want Dougie away from the Libby girl.'

Utah leaned forward. 'Sir, I got no say about Dougie and what he does.'

Blackwell waved his hand. 'I know he's slipping his hand under her dress, and more. Keeps on like this she'll get herself puffed with his bastard offspring. What they share most together is stupidity. I was young myself. You think I don't know about men and their urges for females? Like mongrels sniffing around when a bitch dog is in season. You tell him he's got unlimited credit at the Sip and Dip Saloon and Parlor House. He can have any one of them doves he wants, as many times as he wants. But he's got to quit with Libby Dugan.'

Utah shifted uncomfortably. He was not some nurse-maid for a wild colt with no sense. He took a deep breath and sat straight. 'You want me to remove her?'

'Christ, no, Slaughter. Get Red to help you convince the boy. He's wild and reckless like his mother – her soul rest in peace – never had no responsibility, everything handed to him. I already about given up on him running this ranch and the other business. I'm looking to Red and maybe Jesse to take over when I'm gone, oversee operations for the boy. That is unless I sire another son with a young wife.'

'Like Rebecca Rogers? You been after that almost a year now since her dear loving husband departed.'

Blackwell nodded. 'Taking the buggy to town tomorrow. A picnic. Can you figure a man like me courting, and a damned picnic?'

What Utah could not figure is why the old man didn't just take the bitch and help himself to her property. That was the reason for all this nonsense – her property, the rocky dusty ten acres the late Alfred Rogers, town marshal had bought for her. But Utah sat in the leather chair shaking his head. 'No, sir,' he said. 'Don't figure you tip-toeing around the widow.'

'You wouldn't, would you?'

'I'd help myself to her and everything she has and take no nonsense. You want to marry her property, then you gotta cuff her one, grab her collar, and after you tasted some sweetness, march her straight off to the preacher. That is if you still want to fill her belly with a son. Then

31

everything on her property becomes yours.'

Addison Blackwell leaned back and studied Utah Bill Slaughter. After a full minute, he said, 'That might give pause for consideration.' He had dark hard eyes that showed little kindness.

Something else Utah didn't figure. The widow was maybe thirty or so. What interest did she see in a mean old twist like Blackwell? Was she a little bitch gold-digger after his dwindling wealth? Was she grateful he got rid of her husband for her? One thing Utah knew for certain, Rebecca Rogers had no clue what kind of wealth was on her scrawny land.

Utah said, 'That all you brought me in here for? To straighten out Dougie and get him connected at the Sip and Dip Saloon?'

Blackwell cleared his throat. 'Two of the witnesses from a year ago are getting nervous. Doc O'Connor is telling the marshal he ain't so sure what he saw that night.'

'The town needs a doc, sir.'

'I know, I know. Mebbe just talk to him with force. Convince him what he originally said he saw was right.'

'What about the blacksmith, Sven?'

'A blacksmith is not critical to the town. I know you'd like his wife Inge to become a widow.'

'Could be.' Utah put both hands on the desk. 'But it'll cost you a bonus.'

'I understand.'

'That it?'

'No,' Blackwell said. 'Dougie looks up to you, maybe even wants to be you. Take him along when the assayer comes tomorrow.'

Utah frowned. 'Why? I don't think the kid can keep his mouth shut.'

'We need samples of the ore. I showed you the location.

I'll put the assayer up here at the ranch so he don't have to worry about trespassing.'

'But, sir. Dougie will know. And before I can bust him loose from her, you better figure he'll spill his guts to young Libby. Some men just can't keep shut, got to tell their woman everything, even things that ain't none of their business. Dougie ain't no man and she ain't no woman, so he'd spill even more to her, try to look tall in her eyes. And if he keeps up like he has been, it ain't likely he'll ever get to be a man. I'm telling you, sir, it won't be a good idea to have him with me when we stomp in on the widow's property to steal silver ore samples.'

SIX

Cort Packet saw the drummer wagon before he came to the camp, the camp beside a stream that flowed toward the Rio Grande. It was at least two hours to sundown.

'Hello the camp,' he called.

The wagon carried everything in plain sight from women's dresses to pots and pans. It was pulled by an old grey mule that now munched grass along the stream.

A man came out of the willows with a dainty Derringer-type hide-out gun. 'You here to give trouble?' He was chunky in build and bent, somewhere in his forties, wearing blue wool pants and a sweat-stained yellow shirt with a blue vest. He wore a derby and had beard stubble on his chubby face.

'Just drifting by,' Cort said. 'I bring no trouble.'

'Step on down then. I caught three trout and shot me a rabbit this morning. Willing to share. Got Arbuckle's made and ready, even a jar of moonshine I traded who-knows-where for who-knows-what. Name is Rolling Jack Grey, originally from Joplin.'

'Cort Packet, out of the Texas Pecos a long time ago.' Cort felt pain after he swung down and put weight on the left leg. Too long in the saddle. He pulled the cane and limped to the campfire and sat on a low rock.

'The war?' Rolling Jack asked pointing to the leg.

Cort nodded and took the tin cup of coffee offered. 'Looking for two men might have passed this way, dressed trail dusty and in a hurry. Might have been carrying a jewelry box.'

Rolling Jack had a friendly cherub face that looked slightly painted like an actor. He squinted at Cort. 'Stolen jewelry box? They runners?'

'They are. They stole, raped, murdered and left fire behind.'

'The law after them?'

'What law? *I'm* after them.' He sipped the coffee, which tasted good.

They rolled Bull Durham and lit the smokes from end-burnt campfire twigs. Rolling Jack looked at the cup. He also had a tin cup, but it appeared filled with something other than coffee. 'Care to try some moonshine?'

'Don't mind if I do.' After the gulped coffee, the first swallow of moonshine carried the kick of a mule and boiled Cort's throat going past. The sting was enough to bring tears. 'Lord!'

'I think I got that down Kentucky way. They sure know their mash and liquid boiling. Yup, Cort, I seen your boys. Two days ago. They looked scared as that rabbit I shot, almost like they knew somebody was after them. You figure to shoot them dead when you catch them?'

'I do.'

'Who did they rape and murder?'

'My wife. They pistol whipped my boy to death. He was seven.'

Rolling Jack frowned and shook his head. 'What on earth for?'

Cort blew smoke and took another swallow of the 'shine and looked out across the stream where the shore was lined with willows. Shadows grew long with the setting sun.

'Who knows the why? Got a snoot on, riding wild, come on a small spread with innocents, seemed like the thing to do. She looked too good. The boy was in the way. Burned the house down out of cussed meanness. There were four. I got two of them. You seen the other two. Any sense where they was headed?'

'They talked about a town, a cattle ranch near it where I guess they know some fellas.'

'They give names?'

'No names. One was young, mebbe twenties. The other twice his age. We met on the trail. They only stayed a couple hours. They acted nervous and careful what they spoke about. Yup, they acted ashamed, that's it. They stayed just long enough for some 'shine and to trade. Mebbe they ain't sure it's you, but they talked like some-body was trailing them.'

'Being ashamed won't keep them alive.'

'You want to know what they traded? It was a brooch. Like to see it?'

'No. It'd be part of another life, long gone. What direction did they ride off on?'

'I'd just come from a homestead, the Castro place, Orville and Ada. Traded them a bright yellow dress and ammunition for their Sharps and got a baked apple pie and some buttermilk and hay for the old mule. They got a good garden too. I fairly loaded up on vegetables – onions, corn, radishes, carrots. Ada ain't much to look at, but she's a fine cook.' He shook his head and took another swallow. 'Figure that's homestead life. Ain't no raving beauties living homestead, 'less they're real young. Orville didn't act too happy with Ada on account of she only gave him three girls, no boys.'

Cort said, 'The two fellas you met on the trail headed there?'

36

'Yup, they said they wouldn't mind some down-home cooking. You look troubled, Cort. What you thinking?'

'I'm thinking on how them jaspers might leave the homestead.'

Orville Castro sat on a straight-back chair in front of his shack smoking a corn cob pipe. Ada bustled inside with pans and dishes helped by the two oldest girls looking twelve and ten. The youngest, about Billy-Boy's age, played with a doll in the yard. Cort Packet sat next to Orville, sipping fresh buttermilk, watching the girl and remembering.

'Two days ago,' Orville said. His bib overalls were tattered and filthy. He wore a straw hat and looked evolved from a cornfield scarecrow. Ada and the girls looked no better. The land seemed reluctant to give up its bounty, at least to Orville. Even with the Sharps, he must not have been much of a hunter. The scrawny farm reminded Cort of Ned and Martha's place. Ned Perry was not much of a hunter either. The Castro spread looked only slightly more run down.

'Did you get any names?' Cort asked.

Orville blew smoke up toward the sky. To Cort, the man carried an air of laziness. The wife, Ada, was overworked and underappreciated.

'The oldest jasper,' Orville said, 'looked somewheres around fifty, called hisself Yucca Frazel. He was the quiet one. The other, mebbe twenties, was the loudmouth sweet-talker. Even had Ada smiling. I didn't care for how the young buck looked at my oldest girl. She's only twelve and not quite ready. Anyway, that one says he's Ike Jeffords. They sat the table and ate heavy and quick. Took two helpings of everything. All the time that Jeffords fella eyeballing my twelve-year-old like some hungry sheep-killing wolf. I

37

made them sleep outside. Didn't want that fella anywhere near the house.'

'Did they say where they were headed?'

Orville hawked and spit a gob two feet away into the dirt. 'Not at first. After they ate, no offer to help clean up, left it all to Ada and the girls. No offer to leave anything for the fine meal neither.' He thought silent for a spell. 'When that drummer fella, Rolling Jack Grey come with his wares, I shoulda got a decent dress for the oldest girl instead of Ada. That girl is starting to fill. Mebbe I shoulda got her pants instead. Cover her more.' He shook his head. 'Them girls is going to give me trouble I ain't never known before.' He slapped his leg. 'I need a son, mister. And I don't think Ada is good for any more children. We lost two, girls – died at childbirth – and I jest don't think she'll be able to do her function much longer.'

Mid-afternoon sunshine beat down without shade. Cort tightened his lips, figuring he didn't like the farmer much. He pulled his plains hat and wiped his sleeve across his brow. 'You got no way knowing where they were headed? They mention a place, a town, a ranch, anyplace?'

'Mebbe, mebbe no. You know what that youngest fella, Ike Jeffords, that one did? Just before they left, he give my oldest girl a ring. A fancy ring with a bright green stone. I tell you, Cort Packet, I did not like his attitude. Nothing for me, or for Ada who did all the cooking and serving, but he gives a ring to my oldest just on account of she's so pretty.'

Not once did Orville say the girl's name. Or the name of any of his three girls.

Cort said, 'I'd sure like to know where them two fellas rode off to. If you heard anything, I'd appreciate knowing.'

Orville turned to him. 'You hungry? Want to stay for supper? Ada is a fine cook, for all the other womanly traits she lacks. We're having fried chicken and vegetables from our garden. She makes damn good buttermilk biscuits.'

'Much obliged. But I can't be staying the night, Orville. I got to be heading on down the trail. What did them two jaspers talk about outside the house?'

'Let's eat,' Orville said.

The table was set with mismatched crockery, some of it cracked, and the fried chicken tasted delicious. The three girls, ages twelve, ten and seven, ate quiet. The oldest wore the emerald ring Amanda had brought from Ireland. Orville went at the chicken like it was his last meal. Cort noticed his own plate and cup matched and was without cracks and looked like their best china.

Ada surprised the table by saying, 'Mr Packet, I traded with Rolling Jack Grey for a tin of Chinese tea. Would you like some?'

'Obliged.'

'Do you take sugar, sir?'

'When I can get it, yes'm.'

After the meal and tea were done, Cort gathered his plate, silver, and cup and took them to the sink.

'No need for that, Mr Packet,' Ada said. 'You already got trouble getting around on that leg. I got liniment might ease the pain some.'

Cort was about to speak when Orville said, 'Yup. Come to think on it, them boys sure-nuff said where they was headed. The Yucca fella, he said he had a friend named Jesse something-or-other who worked some big ranch a couple days from here. They did say the name of the town. Unusual on account of how the sunset hit it. I can't recall though. I was so worried about my oldest girl and that young buck it fairly slipped my mind.'

Cort stepped outside putting on his hat. 'Well, Orville, thank Ada for the buttermilk and the meal.' Cort did not figure to get anything more out of Orville. He used his cane and limped to Whiskey who stood saddled in front of the shack.

Orville said, 'They kept looking where they come from like they was scared somebody might catch up to them.'

Ada came to stand in the doorway, wiping her hands with a towel. The oldest girl stood with her arm around her mother's waist. The girl had a petulant, pretty almost-woman face.

Mounted, Cort turned Whiskey so he faced the couple. He nodded to the girl. 'What is her name?'

'Magdalena,' Ada said. 'From the Bible.'

Cort nodded to the girl, then smiled at Ada. 'Mrs Castro, you set an elegant table. Much obliged.' He touched his index finger to the brim of his plains hat and gently heeled Whiskey away.

'Mr Packet,' Ada said. She stepped out of the doorway and moved past the chair where Orville sat on smoking his corn cob. At his saddle, she handed him a small bottle. 'I couldn't spare much, but mebbe even this small amount might ease your pain some.'

'Yes'm, it will, and I do thank you.'

She made a brim of her hand to shadow her face from the setting sun. 'I heard them talking in the yard. The name is Scarlet, sir. The name of the town they rode for is called Scarlet.'

SEVEN

The next morning, the youngest of the two runners, Ike Jeffords, had doubled back and tried to dry gulch Cort Packet. Riding away from the stream along a clump of mesquite and juniper and stagecoach-size boulders, Cort heard the shot and felt the whizz of a bullet zing past his ear. He drew and heeled Whiskey as another shot fired, and the bullet chewed a chunk of juniper bark. Cort rounded a boulder as he pinpointed the jasper's location by the gunfire. He saw Jeffords' horse and thought about dismounting, but he knew he couldn't move around as well on his leg. Jeffords showed himself on top of a boulder thirty feet away, his right shoulder bloodied and bandaged. He looked younger than his twenties. He cocked the hammer of his pistol and aimed. Cort fired two quick shots. One slug hit Jeffords' chest, the other went in his stomach. A head shot would have killed the bastard instantly. Cort did not want that just yet.

Ike Jeffords dropped his weapon and leaned forward over the boulder edge as his boots slipped. He turned enough to claw at the rock, which slowed his slide some, but he still quickly went fifteen feet to the bottom. He slumped in a heap after a series of grunts. Cort dismounted as Jeffords turned onto his back, clutching his belly.

41

'Mister,' he said, 'I been shot up enough now.'

He looked sweaty and dirty and tired. The look of a runner. His golden locks curled loose and covered his ears and neck. His smooth face grimaced in pain. The blue shirt and black vest were soaked with blood. He looked lean and young and filled with terror.

Cort pointed to the shoulder. 'Yucca Frazel do that?'

Jeffords frowned. 'I got him in the hand, the left hand, best I could do. Who are you? What you want shooting me to pieces?'

'Where's Yucca Frazel?'

'He turned on me. Shot my shoulder and took the stuff and lit out.'

'You mean the jewelry box and silverware you stole.'

'How you know that?' His brown eyes went wide. 'Christ, it's you. You been the one after us. It was your place.'

'And my wife you raped and murdered. My son you beat to death. My house you burned.'

His mouth opened. 'No, it weren't like that. You got it wrong, mister. We never seen nobody. We took the stuff and lit off the cabin for spite, but we never seen no wife or boy. We saw you and that other fella shoot down our pards, but never did what you say. There weren't no woman and boy. We seen nobody. You got it wrong, all wrong.'

'Tell the truth, boy, you'll be dead soon enough.'

'You got to help me.'

'Too late. I didn't shoot you in the head because you'd have been done right off. The chest shot mebbe hit a lung. The belly shot speared through your liver. You got less than an hour, and most of that gone. Better clear your soul for your maker.'

Jeffords grimaced in pain. 'I'm sorry we took the jewels and the silverware. I regret we burned up your place. But you can't kill a man for thievery and a fire. You can't.'

With gritted teeth, Cort grabbed a handful of bloody shirt. 'Not for that, you maggot. For rape and murder.'

'No, sir, not such. You got to believe me.'

'You're lying.'

'I ain't, I ain't. You find Yucca, you ask him. We never did nothing like that.'

'Where is this town, Scarlet? That where Yucca went?'

'Scarlet? A day and a half ride west.' His breath came in rasping puffs, quick and shallow. 'How did you get everything so wrong? You go to Scarlet. You look up Yucca, he'll tell you. He's out on the Triangle-B ranch. You ask him. It wasn't us.'

Cort released the liar and stood. He picked up the Remington six-shot and put it in his saddlebag. He looked down at the bleeding man, who lost color in the sunshine. 'Last chance to make peace before you drop to hell.'

But Jeffords was through with conversation, and everything else connected with living.

Cort mounted Whiskey and turned the chestnut west.

The sign at the town limits showed the name, Scarlet and a population of 1,500. What Cort saw in front of him was a dirt-mud main street with boardwalks and clapboard buildings mixed with smaller adobe business huts lining each side. Toward the end of the road, buildings thinned to three tents with wooden floors.

A cow town like hundreds he had ridden through in his past, his past before Amanda and Billy-Boy, a past that caused him to question his value as a man, as a human. It was a past he had ridden back into. The town had been thrown together during the boom when cheap Texas Longhorns might be driven north to trains headed east and sold for double and triple what was paid for them. That had been right after the war when the nation was hungry for beef. The boom played out, as most booms did. Now ranch owners worried about how they would survive while the price of cattle kept dropping. Most sought out another source of income.

While gunfighters like Cort Packet had outlived their time.

A time to sow and a time to reap. And a time to die fallow in the ground, or with your face in the dirt, a six-shooter in your hand.

The sun had started to set. A crimson sky turned the buildings and even the dirt main road a shadowy scarlet, as red as blood. Store windows reflected the color back to the road and across against other windows. For a brief few minutes, the town of Scarlet actually did turn scarlet.

On his right, just beyond the stables, sat a sagging, unpainted, sun-bleached, two-story clapboard building with a bold blue sign that had thick black lettering: Sip and Dip Saloon and Parlor House.

Cort aimed Whiskey for the stables. After his mount was seen to, he pulled the cane and limped toward the swinging saloon doors.

EIGHT

Rebecca Rogers pushed Addison Blackwell's hand down from her bodice and turned her face away from his kiss. 'Please, Addison, no.'

His hand fell to her leg and she felt his grip on it, sliding her dress. 'Becky, you know how I feel about you.'

'I know what you want. And I told you to stop calling me Becky. My name is Rebecca. You show no respect, Addison.'

They sat on a blue wool blanket, a mile out of town, on a grassy knoll beside a stream. The food was done and once again she had to fend the man off. In a moment of weakness two months ago she had allowed his lips to touch hers. He became like a grass fire. When his tongue invaded her mouth, she pushed away and refused to see him for a week. He became like a petulant boy, apologetic with promises it would never happen again unless she wanted it to. And this was from some man at least twenty years older.

Why did she put herself through this?

For information. She was certain her husband Alfred had been murdered a year ago, by at least one other man besides the gunfighter. Somebody in the shadows had fired the instant before Alfred and Utah Bill Slaughter drew on

45

each other. The gunfighter had goaded Alfred with whispered innuendos to insult Rebecca's reputation. That much she learned from two of the four witnesses. Doc O'Connor was one. He now showed doubts about the fair fight he said he saw. Sven the blacksmith had already told her it was not as others had said. He had watched Addison's ranch foreman ride into town late that night and position himself across from the stables. The gunfighter told Sven what to say to the marshal. It had better be the same as the other four. A stable might catch fire with all that hay. Sven was also told he had a pretty Swedish wife and cowhands were always hungry for that sort of thing. But right was right, and Sven was ready to change his statement. He told the marshal he saw Red Jack Wheat fire an instant before Utah Bill did, shooting Alfred in the stomach. The gunfighter worked for Addison Blackwell. Addison had to have known what went on. Rebecca thought if she grew friendly with the ranch owner, she would learn the truth.

Now beside the stream, Addison said, 'How much longer you going to put me off, Becky – Rebecca?'

She sighed. 'I told you I've been unsure.' She squinted at him. 'Are you an honorable man, Addison?'

'It's been a year, girl. You ain't unsure no more. I'm as honorable as any other man you know. Boys and men you knew back home were likely not much more than honorable. The men up north were less about honor and more about fighting. That's why they won. You don't talk no more about honor among men. I want you on my ranch and in my bed.'

'I know you do.'

'You better give me an answer.'

'The answer is the same it has always been. I've already had a husband. He was murdered in this town. I didn't ask

46

you to fix an election to make me marshal, but you made me replace him. I intend to work that position to find out what happened – what *really* happened that night. And I've had complaints from Chief Long Arrow about stolen goods and government issue bad beef. Newt Dugan is stealing from the Mescalero. I intend to catch him at it.'

'Come on, Becky. There's nothing wrong with how Newt runs them heathens on the reservation.'

Rebecca pushed to stand, moving away from his hand on her leg. She brushed the front of her dress. 'I need help. I thought it would come from you since you're so powerful in this town, and you express so much affection toward me. But you aren't helping me.'

Addison rubbed his jaw and squinted out across the stream. He was silent a full minute. His jaw hardened with clamped teeth. 'Yes, it works for me. I figure Christmas is a good time for a wedding. That set OK with you, Becky?'

Rebecca put her hands on her hips and stared at him. 'Are you insane?'

'I'd like June, on account of that ends your marshal job, and you ain't running for re-election. I told you that, didn't I? Thing is, June might not give you enough time to prepare. I know you gals need time when it comes to something as important as a wedding.'

'It's unimportant, mister, because it won't happen, not in June and not at Christmas. Who do you think you are?'

Addison stood to tower over her. He smiled at her. 'You're a wisp of a thing, nice and firm. I like a little more meat on my woman, though, but we can take care of that on down the trail. Your shiny brown hair is too short, but it will grow. Down below your shoulders, I think. I like the mahogany shade of it. You got yourself spoiled growing down south. You been here already two years. You got no plantation now. No parents or siblings. No slave maids to do your bidding. All you ever had here was Alfred who took a young girl like you out of the rubble and made a respectable woman of you. I know you didn't love the man by the stand-off way you acted toward him, but maybe you liked him.' He stepped closer to her. 'Who am I, Becky? I'm not only your husband-to-be, I'm your savior. I gave you the marshal job after Alfred met his end so you'd have that sixty a month to eat and pay for your hotel room. You got nothing else. All I want back is a little affection and to let you run my ranch. You think that's too much to ask?'

Rebecca turned away from him. 'It is an insult.'

'I gave it all to you, Becky – the marshal job, the pay, the badge, the respect they bring. I can just as easy take it away. I got enough push to add you to the soiled doves down at the Sip and Dip Saloon and Parlor House. If you doubt that, just test me. You're a sparrow flying here on a wing and a promise. I own you, girl.'

Rebecca stared up at him, aware that her lower lip quivered. It could not be true. She would not allow it to be true. She had respected Alfred with gratitude. Eventually, she might have loved him. She was the town marshal. But she knew she had lost some of her confidence. Much of what this man told her was fact.

Rebecca said, 'It can't be a June wedding.'

His wrinkled face brightened. 'Christmas it is then. Now, you give me a kiss I can remember.'

When he wrapped his arm around her waist and pulled her body close to him, she pushed her hands against his chest. 'One kiss. Nothing more.'

'Well, maybe for now.'

Rebecca Rogers entered the marshal's office at sundown carrying her double-barrel twelve-gauge shotgun. Her deputies Lucas and Dode waited with their own shotguns.

The buckshot load was to spray in a wide arc. She had hired them and they were closer to her than deputies. She needed them. She could not do the job without them. She knew Lucas and Dode cared for her. They often let her know she was under their protection. Lucas was in his mid-thirties and after the war rode shotgun for the Butterfield line through Kansas and Nebraska, then drifted west. The Butterfield line did not include Scarlet, but a feeder stage-coach came through twice a week. The nearest railroad was a day's ride south toward Santa Fe. Dode was older, just over forty. Yet Rebecca felt a closer bond to him, both from the South. He had been a plantation owner with his parents just outside Atlanta, and had lost them both, plus his slaves, his wife, son and daughter, and all his posses-sions in fire and defeat during Sherman's destructive march through the Southern States. Dode found work riding shotgun for silver mine wagons down in Tombstone and on two occasions was obliged to permanently drop outlaws who attempted a hold-up. Rebecca felt Dode carried obvious romantic admiration for her. He liked to drink beer with his partner Lucas.

'Saturday night,' Rebecca told them. 'Cowhands will be coming to raise hell.'

Lucas wore a tan overcoat that covered his Peacemaker. He had a full black beard and a Montana Peak Stetson. The beard covered his weak upper lip partly shot away in Gettysburg. 'Where you want to warn them, marshal?'

'Let them have their first drink. We'll tell them at the Sip and Dip.'

Dode said, 'Like we do every Saturday night.' Dode wore a grey overcoat and short-brimmed hat. His denim shirt was buttoned to the throat with no collar. He had brown pork chop sideburns whiskered to his cheeks. Two six-shooters stuck in his belt under the coat.

49

Rebecca had put on her deerskin pants and yellow linen shirt. She wore the Southern officer ulster overcoat that had belonged to her father. She thought the pants were too tight. She needed the cowhands' respect if she was to keep order. That respect would not come if they thought she was there to tease. She knew that in towns like Scarlet the amount of respect any woman received depended on how she presented herself. If she dressed provocatively, she would be treated as such. Whether nun or whore, how a woman covered herself determined how she was treated. And she had no way of knowing what Addison Blackwell had told the cowhands. She knew the snickering way of men when it came to talking basics about women, or a woman. He might have said that she was his property and he could have her any time he wished. Or he might have told them nothing, treated them as the hired help they were. She intended to put him off. She had two seasons to get out of her situation, summer and fall. Before Christmas she intended to resolve the killing of her husband, and the Indian agent problem, then be long gone, though she had no idea how.

Dode had been looking out the window. He turned around to face Rebecca. 'Something you ought to know, marshal.'

Rebecca squeaked the desk chair, turning toward him. Out at the back were two barred cells, currently empty. 'What is it?'

'We got us another gunfighter in town. I first heard about him when I was in Tombstone. Even seen him once. He got wounded in the war, carries a cane which don't affect his draw one bit. Fella goes by the name of Cort Packet.'

NINE

Cort Packet stood at the saloon bar watching fifteen rowdy cowhands barge in with a roar of shouts while they bottom-slapped and fondled short flashy skirts. The girls welcomed them because the boys had their pay and were willing to throw it all at them for favors. The town of Scarlet was no Tucson or Tombstone or Santa Fe and the attractiveness of the ladies reflected that. The girls who worked the Sip and Dip Saloon and Parlor House were in their late twenties and early thirties, and plump where they should have been slim. Some had known broken noses and bullet wounds. They wore too much make-up and matched the noise of the men around them and held their own drink for drink.

During the three nights Cort had spent drinking in the Sip and Dip asking questions, he learned that the saloon was owned by Slippery Sheila Calder, a big buxom woman who could have been in her fifties or sixties. She was more than six feet tall and built like a bear. She wore an ankle-length opal-shaded dress that barely held up her obvious assets. Cort did not inquire, nor did he want to know, how she came to be called Slippery. Her voice matched the loudest cowpoke and she ruled everything that went on inside the Sip and Dip with unquestioned authority.

Addison Blackwell was currently seeing the town marshal, a woman called Rebecca Rogers. Mystery surrounded how the previous marshal – her husband Alfred Rogers – had lost a gunfight with a man who worked for Blackwell, Utah Bill Slaughter. Cort had never met Slaughter, but knew of his back-shooting reputation and had crossed shadows with him in the past. As Cort recalled, Utah Bill always liked some kind of edge.

Cort also learned that the rancher's son Dougie courted the seventeen-year-old Libby Dugan and was with her now. Her father Charles ran the mercantile store. A couple of things stood out to Cort. Charles Dugan had acquired a recent majority partner in the mercantile business – Addison Blackwell the rancher. He also had a brother Newt who just happened to be the Indian agent for the valley. Of course, most of the information came from saloon drunks who had little else to occupy their time. Cort was in Scarlet for only one reason: to find and kill Yucca Frazel. If a small-town local gunfighter wanted to step into that, he'd be obliged. As Cort carried those thoughts, Utah Bill Slaughter, dressed in black with silver trim, came through the doorway a few seconds behind the cowhands.

Cort Packet bought a bottle at the bar and took a table in the corner next to stairs, the stairs leading to a balcony flanked by rooms just big enough for a bed and a chest of drawers. At the end of the balcony was the parlor. He poured his glass half-full from the bottle as he glanced around the saloon. Most ladies were up the stairs, occupied. The cowhands who remained drank, talked and waited their turn for a two-dollar poke.

Utah Bill ambled over to his table with an empty whiskey glass. Cort unhooked the rawhide loop on his holster. His back was to the wall. Slaughter had to sit with the crowd behind him.

'Will you share your whiskey, sir?' Slaughter fingered his thin mustache with the fingers of his left hand as he sat. His right hand remained close to his gun belt. The thin pencil growth made him appear more like a gambler than a gunfighter. He also looked older than most gunfighters, with a slight sag to his facial muscles instead of the hard youthful jawline.

The saloon still roared with heavy-drinking cowpokes shouting to be heard. Chairs scraped, a girl squealed then laughed. A piano in the far corner tinkled out a fast happy tune. Cort's table guest turned in his chair as a woman and two men with shotguns entered. They stood just inside the batwing doors, weapons aimed out in an arc. All three wore overcoats, which Cort reckoned covered belly pistols. The woman stood tall and slim with a flat, short-brimmed hat and a marshal badge pinned to the outside of the coat.

The piano stopped silent, which lessened the room noise.

'You boys know the ritual,' she said softly. She aimed her shotgun toward the ceiling and looked about to fire when the room quieted down to church prayer.

After the boys had settled to attention, the marshal said, 'Name is Rebecca Rogers and for you first-timers, I'm the law here in Scarlet. Most of you know my deputies, Dode and Lucas.' She nodded to each in turn. 'I want you to enjoy yourselves, but don't destroy property and no gunplay. I got two empty jail cells and no heartburn filling them up before dawn. You give me a killing and you'll make me mad. I got no more to say.' She and her deputies turned and walked out through the swinging doors.

The roar of voices immediately came back through the saloon.

Slaughter turned back to Cort with a grin. 'Tough little bitch, ain't she? She'll do it, too. I seen her blast away with that twelve-gauge more than once. Both barrels.' He eased a thin cigar from his vest pocket. He offered it to Cort who declined. When Slaughter was lit, Cort pulled his pouch of Bull Durham and started the makings. 'My boss is sweet on her,' Slaughter said.

'How sweet?' Cort asked.

'Sweet enough there'll be a wedding come Christmas. He'll be moving her out to the ranch soon as her marshal job is done. Sometime in June, I'm guessing. I believe he wants her close to grab at when the mood strikes him.' He leaned back in the chair and blew smoke to the ceiling. 'I recall seeing you down around Laredo a couple years after the war, maybe ten years ago. You was walking with a cane then.'

'Still need it sometimes.'

'I took a ball through the shoulder. Gives me some bother now and then. You planning on hanging around, Cort Packet?'

'Just long enough to do what I came for.'

'That'd be Yucca Frazel.'

'It would.'

'Yucca says you're wrong thinking on what he done.'

'How would he know what I think?'

'Rolling Jack Grey, the drummer fella. Yucca and Ike run into him again after they left the Castro place. You remember? The homestead. Them three cute girls? Ike had a feeling for the oldest.'

'Ike is done feeling anything.'

Slaughter stared for a few seconds. 'Yup, I figured. Anyway, Rolling Jack told them who you are and why you were after them. He got real flowery in the spilling of it. Guess he's got a talent for telling a story. Went into a lot of detail. According to Yucca, the story Rolling Jack told scared the living bejesus out of him and Ike. Course they said it weren't true. About the woman, I mean. They took a jewelry box and some silverware and lit a fire. That was it.'

Cort blew smoke and took a sip. 'I reckon Yucca Frazel likes to talk.'

Slaughter smiled. He had a gold eye tooth. 'You mean how come I know so much? He knows you come here to kill him. He gave all they took – the jewels and silverware to our boss. Mr Blackwell has them waiting in a box at the ranch. Mr Blackwell ain't going to sit easy with the killing of his ranch hand.'

'He taking part in stopping it?'

Slaughter sat straight. He took a slow sip of whiskey. 'Let's say mebbe *I'm* stopping it.'

'Mebbe? You are or you ain't. You're not sure?'

'The man is my boss. He says what I got to do.'

The two men sat in silence as the thunder of the crowd roared around them.

A cowhand came barging through the swing doors with a pistol in his hand. His Montana Peak hat covered spring-curled black locks and was slanted to the left side of his head. His young face was flushed with drink. The leather vest covered a blue calico shirt. He looked left to right along the bar then paused a second at the table where Cort and Slaughter sat.

He waved the pistol above his head. 'Where's Sven?' he shouted. 'The bastard cheated me and I'm gonna shoot him dead as a stampeded calf.' He saw the big Swede at the bar push behind another man. 'Fill your hand, blacksmith. Don't nobody else mess in this. We got a shooting coming and Sven is dead.'

Slaughter pushed against his chair. He stood and turned his back to the table and released the thong off the hammer of his Colt Peacemaker. He faced the line of men at the bar.

TEN

Cort Packet watched the movement in front of him. Slaughter's attention appeared to be on the cowhand at the door. He glanced over his shoulder at Cort as he took three side-steps to the left, to have Cort within sight, not behind him. Cort's left hand held the cigarette, his right rested under the table on his Colt.

'Come out from back there like a man,' the cowboy said. He fired a booming shot that hit Sven along the side. The big Swede spun along the bar and glared at the cowboy. 'Sven, I had one loose horseshoe and you give me a bill for all four.'

'*Ja,*' Sven said. 'You needed four. And you come to sniff at Inge, not for no shoe. She tell me that Curly Black fella come snort at her like mebbe you want something.' Sven was barrel-bellied and smooth shaved with no hat and straight blonde hair to his shoulders and carried the smell of horses.

'Inge is too much woman for you, Sven. Get that forty-four in your hand.'

When Sven pulled his belly pistol, Curly Black fired again, missing. Cowhands stumbled over each other getting out of the way. Cigarette, cigar and white gunsmoke hung in the air. The candle chandelier hanging from the ceiling added more dark fog.

Sven fired one shot. The bullet went straight into Curly Black's heart and drove him back to the wall next to the doors where he bumped and dropped his weapon and slid slowly to the floor.

Sven looked around the crowd. 'You see, *ja*? I got to. I got no choice. You all see.'

Slaughter took a step forward. 'Sven, you just killed my saddle pard, Curly Black. Now, you got to pay for that.'

Sven stood in the middle of the room, the pistol still in his hand. 'I got no grouch with you.'

Slaughter pulled the cigarillo from his lips and blew smoke. 'But that's just it, Sven. I got a problem with you on account of you shooting down my friend.'

Sven's gun hand shook. His pale face wrinkled in fear. '*Ja*, you another one come around my Inge. Make dirty talk to her. She tell me. She tell me about that dead fella Curly Black, and she tell me about you. *Ja*, you another one.'

'Are you saying I disrespected your wife, Sven?'

'*Ja*, that's it. You put a hand on her back. Try to go farther. You talk to her in a bad nasty way. *Ja*, you disrespect.'

'Why, I consider that an insult, Sven. I have the deepest respect for your beautiful fine-bodied wife.'

Sven raised his pistol and fired. The bullet chipped a thimble piece of wood out of the leg of Slaughter's chair. Slaughter stood without moving. Sven's flushed face wrinkled with anxiety. He cocked and fired again. A chunk of floor between Slaughter's boots flew away under and behind him. Sven shook his head as if to shake the fear so his aim was better. With speed barely seen, Slaughter drew and fired. The shot was bad and Cort knew why – drew too fast, didn't aim proper. The bullet went in Sven's mouth taking out two bottom teeth and came out just below

Sven's right ear. It missed the brain completely. Sven cocked again. But Slaughter's second shot sent a bullet into the forehead. Sven's head snapped back and he fell like nothing was inside his clothes, like dropped empty rags. He was dead before his face hit the rough-hewed, tobacco-spit-dotted wood floor.

Slaughter holstered his Colt. He turned to face Cort. 'You figure to draw on me, Cort Packet?'

Cort moved his right hand to the top of the table. 'Not tonight,' he said.

At that instant, Marshal Rebecca Rogers and her two deputies slammed through the flapping doors. While the deputies Lucas and Dode angled their aim to the bar, the marshal took one look at the two bodies and fired her shotgun at the ceiling blowing five candles from the chandelier. 'First one heads for a door gets cut in half,' she said, as cowboys stomped out the dropped candle flames.

'Somebody will pay for that,' Slippery Sheila Calder said from halfway down the stairs.

Cort stood behind the table. Five men gathered and carried the bodies out as the marshal moved in front of Utah Bill Slaughter.

'I'll need your weapon, Slaughter,' she said. 'You're under arrest until we get this straightened out.'

Slaughter hesitated. 'You heard the fellas, Marshal. They told you how it went. No need for arrest.'

The marshal aimed her twelve-gauge at his belly. 'Won't be no argument. Lucas, take his weapon.'

Slaughter raised his hands in surrender as Lucas pulled the Colt from its holster.

Cort had seen many saloon killings in his life, with innocent as well as guilty shot dead. His concern was what Slaughter would do next. Standing, ready to pull down if

Slaughter resisted, Cort was aware of two things. For one, Lucas showed no fear or nervousness in pulling the gun-fighter's weapon. The black-bearded man had obviously been there before. He was experienced. And he no doubt had confidence in the power of his shotgun. The second awareness was how lovely the marshal looked up close. Her brown eyes were hard, her shiny brown hair short, but she had high-cheeked features, a perfect mouth and, despite working to look tough, she showed vulnerable soft gestures below the surface. Cort knew the difference between awareness and interest and did not confuse the two. He doubted he would look on the marshal – or any other woman – with personal interest for a long time to come.

Then the brown eyes set on him. 'You're new,' she said. 'Name?'

'Cort Packet.'

Her brow wrinkled. 'Yes, I've heard of you. You're another one like him.' She nodded to Slaughter. Her attention went to Lucas. 'Take Slaughter to the jail. The cells will be full enough come dawn.' She looked up at Cort. 'You're a witness. Maybe you ought to come along too so we can get your account.'

'Some other time.'

She frowned. 'I got another man with a shotgun, you know.'

'And a saloon full of witnesses. I got to be someplace.'

'Where?' she asked.

Lucas appeared amused. He poked the two barrels of his twelve-gauge into Slaughter's belly. 'Kick up a fuss for me, gunslinger. I'm anxious. I ain't pulled the trigger of this here scattergun in four days. I'm overdue.' He pushed Slaughter from the saloon toward the jailhouse.

Cort smiled at the marshal. She really did try to be tough; tried too hard. It didn't suit her.

'You come from the South don't you, Rebecca Rogers. I figure you on a plantation rich with cotton money. All them years ago. Before Yankees run over you and burned you down.'

The marshal kept her frown, but now she blinked. 'I don't figure you from the South.'

'Wasn't. I'm a product of the Texas Pecos.'

'The war was twelve years ago, sir.'

'I see you still live with the punishment of it.'

Now her voice slipped into a slight southern drawl. 'Whatever do you mean, sir?'

'Word around Scarlet is you're a kept woman.'

The marshal swung the shotgun toward Cort. 'You are way off the trail, gunman. You shouldn't listen to the babble of saloon drunks. I don't want to march you off now. You best get out of this saloon. Find a hole someplace to crawl into. And think about leaving town real soon.'

ELEVEN

Pushing toward midnight, Cort Packet needed the cane to get up to Doc O'Connor's office. The office was above Scarlet Mercantile which was owned by Charles Dugan, who had a majority partner named Addison Blackwell and the Indian agent brother, Newt. Cort wanted everybody in his memory slot so he remembered them.

With the thump of the cane on stairs, the back door of the mercantile below flew open and a young man and young woman scurried out, the man jumping as he ran with one pant leg on. Cort watched them run behind the tent next door. In the moonlight, they both looked like youngsters, certainly under twenty. The rancher's son and Libby Dugan? Cort thought he heard the boy's name was Dougie.

A window was at the top of the stairs. Cort looked through to see a man at a desk with a half-empty bottle of bourbon in front of him. He looked shadowy in the weak lantern light. Cort lightly knocked on the door.

'It is not locked,' a voice said from inside.

Cort went in. The office and clinic were one twenty-foot room. A waist-high rolling bed had been pushed against a far wall. Above the bed was a cabinet filled with lotions, potions and pills of one kind or another. Three armchairs were positioned around the room. The doc's surgical tool pouch sat on the bed. Doc O'Connor was on one side of the desk, an empty chair on the other. A regular unmade single bed was pushed against the wall next to the door behind an open white curtain. There were three lanterns, with only one lit now. The doc waved to the chair opposite him and Cort sat.

Cort leaned the cane on the arm of the chair and pulled Bull Durham makings from his vest pocket. 'Evening, Doc.'

Doc O'Connor appeared to be in his early sixties. His white hair thinned enough to show mostly pink scalp. His eyebrows were thick and glaring-white, even in the weak glow of the desk lantern. He wore rectangle spectacles with thin wire frames. He had a small mouth and needed a shave. His stare was direct and did not waver.

'Who are you?' he asked.

'Cort Packet from down Pecos way.'

The doc nodded. 'You having trouble with the leg?'

'No more'n usual. It acts up from time to time.'

'Want me to look at it?'

'That ain't why I'm here, Doc.'

Doc O'Connor pulled back a desk drawer and drew out another glass. He held the glass up toward Cort. 'Interested?'

Cort had lit his cigarette. 'Don't mind if I do.'

With a pour and a sip from his own glass, the doc leaned back. 'Why are you here, Cort Packet from the Pecos in Texas? I already told the marshal I'd change my story about what happened that night. There was one other shooter, not two. With Sven changing his view, the law should be convinced of what really happened. Unfortunately, Sven is no longer with us.'

'It ain't about that,' Cort said. 'I'm here about Yucca Frazel. I figure he come to you about two, three days back.'

'With a shot hand, yes. I stitched it up and sent him on his way.'

Cort sipped smooth bourbon, much better than what he was used to swallowing. 'His left hand. You get a take on if he's right- or left-handed?'

'His holster was on his right hip. I assume he is right-handed.'

'Then the wound won't affect his draw.'

'You thinking of killing the man, Mr Packet?'

'Yes sir, I am. Tonight if I get to him.'

'Mr Blackwell does not hold kindly to having his ranch hands shot to death.'

'That ain't in my corral. Now I know Frazel's draw ain't affected, I can go at him direct.'

Doc O'Connor shifted in his seat. He poured more bourbon in his glass and added some to Cort's. 'I don't know what Yucca has done, but maybe you should go to the marshal with this.'

'It went beyond the law. It's something personal. Has to do with rape and murder.'

'Oh, my. Come to think about it, Marshal Rebecca Rogers already has enough to think on.'

'You mean like being a kept woman?'

'That is a push, Mr Packet. She's hardly being kept, despite what drunks at the Sip and Dip say. She confides in me and I am not sharing what we talk about. She has not succumbed to anyone, no matter how rich and powerful. But the woman feels pressure from all sides, bombarded whichever way she turns. Too much is going on around her that she feels is beyond her capability. She knows she should never have taken the marshal job. She knows it and I know it. But she's determined to find the truth of what happened to her husband.'

'You ever ask her what she wants?'

'I know what she wants. She and I both believe she will not find it in Scarlet.'

'Like I said, Doc.'

'I know. It ain't in your corral.'

'I'm just here to take care of Yucca Frazel, then I'll be on down the trail.'

'To where? To what?'

'Ain't nothing I thought about.'

'You should see bone specialists in San Francisco about that leg. They are doing good things now, many advances since the war. I used to be good at research for human bone ailments.' He took more than a sip, a gulp that emptied the glass. 'I used to be good at many things, in another life.'

As Cort Packet rode Whiskey along the dark road to the Triangle-B ranch, he reckoned this was a good time. Most of the ranch cowhands were in town raising hell. Absent from them were the owner, ranch foreman, wounded Yucca Frazel and his sidekick, Jesse Ryan. Cort never did get the foreman's name. There were enough of them to go around. He hoped he wouldn't have to equalize the number and could just deal with the one rapist-killer who also liked to steal and set fires.

Moonlight made the arch over the road just visible enough to read. It was a triangle with a block B in middle, an open gate in the barbed-wire fence. About fifteen Longhorns stood silent, some grazing on grass. More cattle were within sight. Cort rode another hour before he saw the ranch house and surrounding buildings. Lantern light showed from the window of the main house.

Cort stopped Whiskey at the hitch by the front door. 'Hello, the house.' He had his Colt ready to slip from its holster in one motion.

A silence of almost a minute greeted him. Shuffling of feet from inside followed, then a man's voice said, 'I got weapons if you're here to be hostile.'

Cort remained mounted. 'No need for weapons unless you're Yucca Frazel.'

'I ain't, but he works for me. You must be Cort Packet, come to do killing.'

'I am. You figure to have me dry gulched?'

The front door opened. The man looking early to late fifties was in shirt sleeves with no boots. His thinning hair was mussed and he looked bone weary, like a man who badly needed sleep but could not get to it for whatever reasons he fed himself. He held a Civil War Remington in his right hand.

'Addison Blackwell,' he said. 'Step down, come in. I know who you are and what you want.' The Remington pointed down along his right leg. Once Cort dismounted and tied Whiskey to the rail, he followed Blackwell through the doorway and down a short hall that led to a book-furnished den with a big oak desk. 'I got good bourbon from Kentucky. Want a cigar, Mr Packet?'

'Got my Bull Durham.'

They sat opposite from each other with the oak desk between. Cort noticed a box the size of a small saddle on the floor to his left at the end of the desk.

Blackwell put the Remington on the blotter in front of him and pointed at the box. 'Everything they took, Mr Packet. Jewelry box, silverware, gold pieces.' He poured bourbon into a glass and slid it to Cort. 'It's all there, everything.'

Cort sipped the good bourbon while he squinted at the box. 'Not quite everything, mister. Where is Yucca Frazel? I want to settle this tonight.'

'What makes you think he won't try to dry gulch you on

a road or trail?'

'His partner already tried.'

Blackwell nodded then tightened his lips. 'Packet, I can't let you gun down one of my cowhands. I *won't* let you. The box has most of what was taken. My boys did not do anything to your wife and boy.'

'And you know that 'cause they told you so. At least, Frazel did. You ain't got no other boys around to lie no more.'

Blackwell shook his head. 'Not my boys. Yucca had a sick ma and went home to tend her. I knew Ike, but not the other two. Yucca must have picked up with them on the trail. Got bad influenced by them to raid your place.'

'Where is Yucca Frazel?' Cort pulled the makings and had another sip of bourbon before rolling a cigarette. 'He at the bunkhouse?'

Blackwell sighed. 'I got him and Jesse working cattle from a canyon far to the north. It's hidden good enough you won't find him any time soon. He didn't do what you say. You're at *my* ranch and Scarlet is my town. I'm asking you, Cort Packet. Take the box and ride out.' He placed his hand on the Remington. 'For now, I'm asking. You don't listen, I'll be telling you in a way you won't forget. You pursue this thing with Yucca, you just get yourself a belly full of trouble.'

'Trouble is what I come looking for,' Cort said. 'That and Yucca Frazel.'

TWELVE

For Utah Bill Slaughter, two saddlebags filled with sample ore was enough for the man at the ranch house. The silver vein was visible and started out thick as a man's arm. By the look of it, by the time the silver was followed to become a cave, the vein might be wide as a horse. That could make it as big a strike as Bisbee or Tombstone, or even Virginia City. He heard the voice sounds of scrawny, skinny Dougie halfway down the rocky hill, making pistol shot sounds as he practised his cross-draw.

Utah slung the saddlebags across his shoulder and looked down the hill. Their horses waited at the bottom. 'You forget why we're here?'

Dougie turned to him, the shiny Colt Peacemaker .45 still in his hand. 'Damn, I'm fast. You see that, Utah, see how quick I can draw? Bring on *all* them young gunslingers. Old has-beens too. I tell you I'm so fast I scare myself.'

Utah came down the hill studying the youngster. He didn't see what the Libby girl saw – loose-fitting canvas pants, fancy inlaid boots, a flowery blue-yellow shirt with brown silk vest, a Montana Peak hat. The kid had a partly pimpled face and the cold dark eyes of his pa – hard to tell a color – and the thin mouth, with a nose too big for his triangular cheeks. He was stoop-shouldered and hollow-chested. And the kid was cocky, which at nineteen did not leave many more years of life in him. His oats were sown spreading seed to Libby, and that made him overconfident because Libby was a pretty seventeen-year-old girl, and every cowhand at the ranch knew she could do so much better. Why she chose Dougie to give herself to was the mystery of the bunkhouse.

Dougie holstered the Peacemaker and followed Utah to the horses.

Utah tied the saddlebags to the back of his saddle. 'The assayer is waiting. We best be getting back. You thought any more on what I said?'

'I ain't getting rid of my girl, Utah. I don't care what Pa or you say. She's too sweet and feels too good, and I know I'm the only one, the one and only, and the first one.'

'You can dip your wick in any pretty bit of fluff at the Parlor House.'

'Whores. They's all whores. Even the two at sixteen and seventeen been wore out.'

'That ain't something you wear out, boy. You just leave it alone for a spell. Come back to it, it's just as sweet as before.'

'Not sweet as my Libby.' Dougie spun back with a draw. 'Yes, sir, I fairly do scare myself.'

Utah sighed, looking at the boy, the kid, the scrawny juvenile slow thinker. 'Can you hit the side of a mountain?'

Dougie stood tall and pulled his shoulders back. 'Damned if I don't think I'm just as fast as you. Come on, let's stand side-by-side and find out. Pa should send me after that new man, that gunfighter come to town to kill poor Yucca Frazel. Bet I could take the jasper. Come on, Utah, side-by-side, see who's faster.'

'I already know who's faster.'

The kid's face scrunched up like he was ten. 'Aw, come on, Utah. Let's find out.'

Utah faced Dougie. 'Why do you have a cross-draw?'

'I seen a fella with it once. It looked slick as a snake's belly. And I'm so fast, so damned fast.'

'Stand tall. Go for the draw while I count.'

Dougie stood tall, his face locked in a mean expression that looked ridiculous. He put his hands to his sides. 'Ready.'

'Go. One-two-three-four.'

Dougie had the Colt in his hand aiming at Utah. 'Four seconds, that's fast, ain't it?'

'Fast enough to get you killed. See, what you got to do is reach up, slide your hand across your belly, grip the Colt, then pull it out of the holster, swing it around to aim, cock and fire. Takes too long.' He stepped close to Dougie. 'Let's slide the gun belt so the holster is high on your hip.'

'You mean like yours, and some others.'

'Not too low. The butt should be even with your wrist. Now, as you raise your hand, you immediately have a grip. As the Colt clears the holster you got it cocked. Swing it up, aim and pull the trigger.' He stood and sighed. 'And hope you hit what you're aiming at.'

'I can take that gunfighter, that Cort Packet fella. I know I can.'

Utah looked back up the hill where the pick had broken the land. He envisioned wagon load after wagon load of silver ore rolling out for processing. He looked back at Dougie. 'You better steer clear of Cort Packet. You'll live longer.'

'But I can back you up when you take him. Tell me I can back you up, Utah, like Red did with the marshal.'

Utah and Dougie mounted. Utah said, 'Don't be flapping your tongue about that too much. I still got to have a talk with Doc O'Connor, get him to stick with the story we told him.'

Dougie grinned at him. 'You mean before you go to visit Sven's widow, Inge? Something clean and pure about them Swedish gals. You got a lot of competition with that one, Utah. Wouldn't mind having a sample myself.'

Utah looked straight ahead as they walked their horses. 'If it ain't overconfidence in your draw, it will be your flapping mouth. One of them is liable to get you killed real soon, Dougie.'

Utah figured the assayer, Mr Blue, got so excited he might pee himself. Mr Blue had never seen silver ore so pure. It was the richest find he had ever been involved with. Since the feeder stagecoach run didn't roll into Scarlet until tomorrow, the gent would have to spend another night. He wanted to go into town, maybe visit the Sip and Dip saloon, go upstairs to the Parlor House and sew some oats. Mr Blue had a wife and five noisy girls back home in Santa Fe. He allowed as how once the mining started and word got out it would be hard to keep all that silver a secret. The assayer looked mousy and wife-dominated, especially being outnumbered by females. Out on the road like he was, he acted like he wanted to whoop and holler a bit. Utah didn't understand completely. He knew the need for a woman different than the one at home, not better so much as just different. Utah had never been dominated by any woman so that part he didn't understand.

What Utah thought about mostly was getting his hands on as much of that silver ore as he could. Maybe he might force the widow to sell the property to him. He was sure Blackwell had already tried that. She might have been slim and tidy, but she was feisty. And she had those two shotgun deputies with her, always. Utah never figured any wedding would come off. The silver would have to be stolen. And Utah intended to get a big share before everything got all complicated and legal. Dougie might be a problem because he'd been there when Utah got the sample ore. The thing to do was let fast-draw Dougie learn he wasn't quite so fast as he thought and make poor little Libby a widow before she became a wife. It wouldn't be hard. The marshal didn't like Cort Packet much. Almost anybody might shoot the overconfident kid down and blame it on the gimpy gunman. It could be done late at night like it was with the previous marshal.

Addison Blackwell called in Red Jack Wheat to take Mr Blue to town. He told Utah to ride along and look after the assayer. Wouldn't do for the gent to fall into the wrong hands and get himself hurt. And it wouldn't do for the gent to get drunk and start shooting off his mouth about silver and where it was located. While in town, Utah might have his talk with Doc O'Connor, and of course visit the widow Inge. If Utah happened to run into the gunfighter looking for a pack mule and supplies for a back-canyon ride, well who knew what kind of hostilities might break out between gunmen. Tomorrow, Blackwell was going to visit the other widow in town, Rebecca. Now he knew for certain how rich the property was, no need to wait all the way to Christmas for a wedding. If Rebecca Rogers didn't think herself ready, Blackwell told Utah, he'd make damned certain she *got* herself ready.

As a final order, Addison Blackwell told Utah to take Dougie with him. While in town he could finalize the breakup between Dougie and Charles Dugan's daughter, Libby.

THIRTEEN

Cort Packet woke in his hotel room sweating with the nightmare. He didn't think the battlefield even had a name, just some unknown skirmish in a forgotten field, close to the end, 1865. The Yankees had five cannons set fifty feet apart, aimed low, firing steel balls in a can of gunpowder. The smoke of gunfire dominated the field making it hard to see anything. Cort felt the ball shatter his leg which sent him rolling and he momentarily blacked out. When he came around he barely made out the cannon and the eight Yankees loading and firing through the smoke. Cort had crawled and fired, killing four. Two ran. He shot the two remaining as they were about to fire the cannon again. The last two were boys, the youngest on his back gagging with vomit and blood splattering over his face. Cort began to shake as the two boys stiffened and were silent. This was what his war had come to. He continued to shake – as he shook now on the bed – until the retreat was sounded.

Cort sat against the bed headboard covered in sweat, letting his breathing slow. He tried to push the scene from his thoughts, but it went with reluctance. Once he replaced it with the image of Amanda close to him, he began to relax. He had quit drinking and fighting and killing only because of her. The quiet life never really sat completely comfortably with him, though she made it work, and parts of him would miss the soft feel of it. The boy helped it along, making Cort devoted. But after that life got beaten and murdered and burned away from him he felt only vengeance – the need for revenge and dealing it out the old way, the only way he knew how, with the gun. If necessary he would draw down on Utah Bill Slaughter, after he put bullets into Yucca Frazel. He would gun down the ranch owner and his brat kid, even the town marshal if she got in his way. If it all came to a final showdown, he would even level and burn the burg to its namesake – Scarlet, with the flames of revenge.

After breakfast at the hotel café, Cort limped outside lighting his rolled Bull Durham. Across and down the street, Utah Bill Slaughter stepped down the stairs from the doc's office, licking the knuckles of his right hand. He hadn't noticed Cort because he was looking down toward the entrance to the Scarlet Mercantile where Charles Dugan waited outside. They spoke and both went inside the store.

Cort crossed the street and climbed the stairs using his cane. He knocked on the door. When no response came he went in. Doc O'Connor was stretched on his bed by the door. His face looked bruised and had started to swell.

Cort said, 'Did he convince you?'

'What? What?' The doc frowned. One lens of his spectacles was cracked. 'Who are you? What do you want? Wait. You're Cort, Cort Packet.'

Cort slid a chair and sat next to the bed. 'Did Slaughter convince you to keep to the old story about Slaughter and the marshal and nobody else?'

The doc blinked hard. 'Don't ask me that. Please don't ask.'

'Can I get you anything?'

'The cabinet over there. Bring me the bottle of pain easing powder. Nothing is broken but I have a terrible headache.'

Cort fetched the powder. He poured water into a glass and added a couple teaspoons of the powder. 'There you go.'

'Bring me the bottle in the desk drawer.'

'Not just yet. What did you see that night a year ago?'

The doc blinked. 'A draw between the marshal and Utah Bill Slaughter. Slaughter was faster and the marshal was killed.'

'How many shots?'

'Two.'

'Who was waiting in the shadows across from the stables?'

'Nobody.' The doc covered his eyes with his hand. His glasses fell off. 'I can't. I know they'll kill me.'

'Who was it? You already told the marshal once. She won't let you go back on your word.'

His hand came away. 'It was Red. He fired first as they drew.'

'Red who?'

'The ranch foreman, Red Jack Wheat. Don't you know him?'

'The only name got me riled is Yucca Frazel. I got me a mule so in the morning I pack and go deep to the canyons.'

The doc swallowed from the glass. 'You may not need to go packing.'

'Why so?'

'I told Yucca before he left he had to look after that hand. Keep it clean. Change the bandage every day. I told Jesse and I told Yucca. Sure enough, they didn't listen. Now

75

it looks like infection might be setting in. The hand has started to swell.'

'So, he's coming back to see you.'

'One of the ranch hands told me.' The doc sat on his bed. 'I really should get to that bottle.'

'In a minute, Doc. When do you expect him?'

'Jesse is bringing him in today or tomorrow. They may swing by the ranch first. The cowhand said it might be at night on account of they know you're in town ready to kill Yucca. I don't think the marshal knows that. But Addison Blackwell and his boy Dougie, and Utah Bill Slaughter and Jesse Ryan reckon that's the only reason you're in town. But everybody is just guessing. Men say things that float like passed gas in the wind. You don't deny it.'

'Then it must be true,' Cort Packet said.

FOURTEEN

When Cort stepped out of the doc's office, he watched the marshal come toward the front of Scarlet Mercantile. She was flanked by her two deputies. All three still wore their overcoats with their shotguns at the ready. They entered the store and the sound of shuffling feet followed.

Cort went down the stairs and into the store. Merchandise to supply most life needs were stacked and piled up. Utah Bill Slaughter and another man talked close behind the counter. The man wore a shop apron and no hat. He looked in his forties and not pleased that the marshal and her deputies were there. He was portly but taller than the marshal. He wore a green shop apron. Cort reckoned the man to be the owner – part owner, Charles Dugan. A girl stacked bolts of cloth in the corner. She appeared slim with big bright blue eyes and blonde hair to the small of her back – the daughter, Libby. She looked at Cort and smiled as if flirting with him. It was that kind of smile. A smile too experienced for her young age.

Slaughter was saying, 'Marshal, what brings you in here? Come to look at cloth for a wedding dress?'

Cort looked from one to the other. The deputies, Lucas and Dode, stood apart at each side of the door.

The marshal said, 'I'm here to check your inventory, to

see if any merchandise is from the agency.'

Charles Dugan came around the counter to stand over the marshal. 'Now, Marshal, you got no need for that. And you ain't got the clout. That there Indian agency is government business. You ain't even a county sheriff. Just a little town marshal. Why don't you find some cloth over there for a nice wedding dress? Libby will help you. Libby?'

Slaughter stared at Cort. 'What you doing in here?'

Cort reached for change in his vest pocket. 'A pouch of Bull Durham,' he said to Charles Dugan. He touched the brim of his hat. 'Marshal. Rebecca, isn't it? Rebecca Rogers?'

The marshal gave him a passing glance without expression and to Dugan said, 'Charles, the inventory. I want a look in your back room.' She turned back to Cort. 'I thought I told you to leave town. Why are you still here?'

Cort smiled at her. He looked at Dugan. 'The Bull Durham?'

Dugan pulled a pouch and put it on the counter. He took Cort's change. He looked steadily at the marshal. 'You ain't got the authority to look in my back room.'

'My deputies are holding my authority.'

Slaughter blocked the opening. 'I wouldn't advise this, Rebecca.'

Cort took a step forward. 'I reckon it will be all right.'

Slaughter and Cort stood facing each other. Rebecca blinked at Cort.

Slaughter said, 'You want it here in a hardware store?'

'Why not? You got nobody hiding in a closet, do you? Nobody to dry gulch and help you along? We can put your carcass in one of them wheelbarrows over there.'

'What do you mean by that?'

'You chew on it awhile.'

'That's enough,' the marshal said. 'You two can decide

who has the biggest shooter some other time, some other place. Utah, stand aside. I'm going in that back room. Lucas? Dode?'

The deputies stepped forward, their shotguns aimed at Slaughter and Charles Dugan. In the corner, Libby watched with her mouth open. Her face showed uncertain confusion.

Cort stepped back to give the marshal and the deputies a clear passage. With a parting look at Utah Bill Slaughter, he noticed a change in Slaughter's expression. Slaughter stared at the two deputies. He stared at them with a loathing hatred, his right hand close to his holster.

The five men and the young girl stood silent for the five minutes the marshal searched the back room. When she came out she had two ledgers under her arm. 'I'll just be looking through these.' Her deputies backed away.

Charles Dugan said, 'You found nothing, right. I knew you wouldn't. You better leave me them books. I'm going to report this invasion to the Indian agent.'

'You mean your brother. Go ahead.'

Cort said to the marshal, 'Not here, Rebecca. You ain't going to find nothing here or likely in those books. You got to go there, to the reservation. That's where government property is shipped.' He nodded to Dugan. 'By the time it gets here, this one already has it marked and priced as bought stock. It won't show on no lading bills or receipts, or them books. Check his paperwork at the time, then.'

'That won't be allowed,' Dugan said.

The marshal looked from Dugan to Cort then back to Dugan. 'It will to a federal marshal. I got one coming. He'll be here in a week.'

'Too late,' Cort said. 'This one will have cooked the books by then.'

Dugan stepped forward with a frown. 'Who the hell are

you, mister, messing in my business?'

Slaughter said, 'He's a gunslinger like me, here to gun down Yucca Frazel. And who knows who else?'

Dugan still stared at Cort, his lips tight. 'Stay outta my business.'

Cort turned to Slaughter but spoke to Dugan. '*Your* business, Dugan? Word is you got a powerful majority partner, likely come in without an invite.' He turned to glare directly at Dugan. 'You and your brother are sliding down a well.'

The marshal put her hand on Cort's arm. 'Do you have proof about this partner?'

'I ain't in the proof business, Marshal, I'm in the justice business.'

The marshal's soft brown eyes studied him. 'You figure to give hard justice to Yucca Frazel?'

'Could be.'

She hardened her look. 'Better think about it. You best leave now. If you know something about this, you better come by the office. I'd like to hear more on what you know. About this store and so-called partners.'

Lucas and Dode backed to the door and waited for the marshal.

Slaughter said, 'He don't know nothing, Rebecca. He only hears the babble of drunks over to the Sip and Dip.'

The marshal looked from Cort to Slaughter. 'What gives you men the right to call me by my name? None of us are friends. To you, I'm the marshal. Address me that way.' She nodded to Charles Dugan. 'We'll talk again, real soon.'

Dugan gave her a smile that held no humor. 'Sure, Marshal. You be sure and let me know when that federal man shows up.'

As the marshal moved to the door with her deputies, Slaughter grinned at her with a possum-eating face 'Be seeing you around, Becky.'

*

Cort returned to his hotel room to rest for what he reckoned would be an event-filled night. With an infected hand, Yucca Frazel would ride in to see Doc O'Connor. Cort could watch the stairs to the doc's office from the front porch of the hotel. He lay on the hotel room bed, unable to close his eyes. For one, the nightmare might come back. For another, Frazel might sneak in and out without getting himself shot for his deeds. And his pard, Jesse Ryan would be with him.

After supper, Cort had two drinks at the Sip and Dip, then with a pint bottle of whiskey under his vest, he found a chair on the hotel boardwalk and sat to wait. He knew where the important people were. Utah Bill Slaughter was up the street visiting with the widow Inge. Marshal Rebecca Rogers had ridden to the Indian agency, but was back at her office with her deputy, Dode. The other deputy Lucas was making the rounds, checking stores and action inside the Sip and Dip. The boy Dougie Blackwell was sparking somewhere with Libby Dugan. A stranger was in town, a Mr Blue who came in from the Triangle-B with Red Jack Wheat, the foreman. Word spread Mr Blue had something to do with silver. Speculation began among the saloon drunks as to where anyone would find silver around Scarlet.

Shortly after midnight, Yucca Frazel and Jesse Ryan rode to the doc's office. Not one minute later a ruckus stirred up in the inky darkness behind the Sip and Dip. The deputy Lucas Price shouted with another man, but the words could not be made out. Gunshots split the night and word spread rapidly that the deputy was shot dead, in the back.

81

FIFTEEN

The showdown between Cort Packet and Yucca Frazel happened at the bottom of Doc O'Connor's stairs next to the Scarlet Mercantile.

Using his cane for support, Cort limped towards the two men, a finger pointed at Jesse Ryan. 'Unless you want a piece of this, better step off.'

The two men had just swung down off their mounts.

Jesse Ryan stood in front of Yucca Frazel. 'Don't do this, mister. The man is in pain.'

'Look how swelled my hand is,' Frazel said. He cowered behind his pard, knees shaking. He was a cross-draw with the holster over his belly. He looked at Cort with pleading eyes. 'You got this wrong, mister, completely wrong. We give you back your things. What you think happened with your wife wasn't us. We didn't do it. You got to believe me, pard. It weren't us. We was drunk and just wanted to raise a ruckus some. Yup, it was wrong, us burning your house and all, and taking your things. But we didn't do what you think.'

He looked older than Cort expected. Aged by living every day seeing the infection – lack of appetite and little sleep wrinkled his face more. He was maybe in his fifties, but creased and bent. Now ready to cry as he spat out his lies. Few men walked comfortably with what they had done.

Jesse Ryan was about the same age. He had a face that had been hit by just about everything. He dressed cowboy, Montana Peak hat, huge red kerchief, open cowhide vest, canvas pants, and worn unpolished lopsided boots that didn't like walking on ground. He looked like he should be with a herd someplace, riding the range.

'I'm hurting,' Frazel said. 'My hand got itself infected.'

'Step aside,' Cort told Jesse Ryan. 'This has waited long enough.'

Jesse Ryan stayed put.

The door at the top of the stairs opened and Doc O'Connor came out, peering over the top of his wire spectacles with the bottle in his hand. 'Better let him come up, Mr Packet.'

'The hand won't matter,' Cort said.

Jesse Ryan moved toward the stairs. 'Come on, Yucca. He won't shoot you in the back.'

Frazel turned away and clutched the wrist of his injured hand. He came back around with the Colt out of its holster. Cort had already drawn and now fired. The first shot chunked away Frazel's chin, tore it away from his face. A second shot went in the temple as Frazel stumbled sideways and went down to one knee. His Colt dropped to the dirt. The gunshots echoed off the dark walls of Scarlet. Cort shot him again in the chest, then swung his Peacemaker to Jesse Ryan.

'Don't,' Cort said. 'Or you'll join him.'

Ryan's face wrinkled in a frown of despair. His hand stretched out away from his holster. 'No, aw no, you done killed him. You went and shot him dead.' He left the stairs and knelt next to the body. 'After the war we rode against Missouri and Kansas banks, taking Yankee cash for what they done to us and ours. All them years on the trail together. We seen a lot of country, shared too many camp-fires. And it comes down to this.'

'You want revenge?' Cort asked.

Ryan looked up at him. 'Against you? A professional gunman?' He shook his head. 'My killing days ended long ago, mister. But you're wrong about what those boys done.'

'You weren't there,' Cort said. 'You didn't see what they left. You don't know.'

Jesse Ryan looked down and shook his head. 'Completely wrong.'

From the top of the stairs, Doc O'Connor said, 'Here comes the marshal.'

Cort Packet was put in a jail cell that smelled of stale beer and puke. Marshal Rebecca Rogers took statements from the doc and Jesse Ryan. No question Yucca had drawn first and the gunfighter was just defending himself. Looking on the verge of tears over the back-shooting of her deputy, the marshal unlocked and opened the cell door.

'Mr Packet, you now have no reason to stay in town,' she said.

Cort strapped on his gun belt. 'Lucas gone, you're out-gunned in this town, Marshal.'

'With two gunfighters I am. But you'll be gone now. You've done what you came here to do. Unless you two gunmen draw down on each other.'

'No,' Cort said. 'You got more than the loss of a deputy to buck up against. You got the ranch owner Blackwell to deal with. Besides his romantic intentions toward you, he's the majority partner at the mercantile. You got Charles Dugan stealing government property from the Apaches, with help from his brother.'

'Newt Dugan,' the marshal said.

Cort nodded. 'You got Utah Bill Slaughter who's

messing his hand in a lot of pies. He killed Sven and now helps himself to the widow. I'm sure that ain't with her consent. If Inge has any gumption she'll do something about it.'

The marshal handed Cort his hat. She went behind the desk and sat in the chair. She frowned at him. 'What did Yucca Frazel and his riding pals do to you? I know they burned down your place and stole a jewel box and silver-ware. That wouldn't be reason enough to hunt them down and kill them. Why, Cort?'

'They caved in the skull of my son, Billy-Boy, and pistol-whipped him to death. They raped, beat and murdered my wife, each taking a turn. They paid now, every last one of them.'

Rebecca blinked away tears. 'You have so much hate in you.'

Cort turned for the door. He looked back. 'How did Lucas get it?'

'Shot in the back from darkness behind the saloon.'

Cort had his hand on the doorknob. 'You know who operates like that. Where was Slaughter?'

'With Inge, the widow. She swears it, not in talk, with head nodding. She doesn't speak the language well.'

'If not Slaughter, that leaves the other shooter to kill your husband a year ago.'

Rebecca sighed deep. 'Yes, Red Jack Wheat. But proof, Cort. I have no witnesses, no evidence, no proof.'

Cort opened the door. 'He ought to be shot down where he stands.'

'Don't go on a rampage. You want to be my deputy?'

'I wouldn't stand comfortable with a badge pinned on me.'

'Then don't wear a badge.'

Cort stood at the open door. Faded crowd noise reached

him from the Sip and Dip toward the end of the block next to the stables. In back of the stables was the small cabin where Inge lived and her constant visitor helped himself. The visitor would have to be dealt with.

'I might poke around some,' he said.

'You aren't going home?'

Cort paused. 'Amanda and the boy were my home. With them gone, I got no place to go. Where did Red Jack Wheat say he was when Lucas got himself back shot?'

'With a Mr Blue, the silver man, inside the Sip and Dip. He said they were upstairs in a private room talking silver business.'

'Where is there any silver around here?'

Rebecca shrugged. 'Maybe somewhere on the Triangle-B.'

Staying inside, Cort closed the door. 'What you intend to do about the rich ranch owner panting on you?'

Rebecca cleared her throat. 'Will you be my deputy, Cort?'

Cort leaned on the doorknob. 'No. You ain't got long to be marshal anyway, do you?'

'A month to go. June. Rumor has it I'm to be a bride in June. I thought it was going to be Christmas, but something jumped it all ahead.'

'You running for re-election.'

'Not the longest day I live. No matter who says different.'

'What will you do?'

'Didn't you just hear me?'

'You ain't gonna be no bride. No way anything will twist that way.'

'Why not? You going to stop it?'

'Nope, you are.'

'And what are *you* going to do?'

'Reckon I might stay around a spell. Some things in this hiccup of a place need looking after.'

'Like me?'

'You'll be fine with a little help, Marshal. Unless you run me out of town, I might make a pest of myself to certain bad *hombres*.'

Rebecca leaned back in the chair. 'Nobody is running you anywhere, Cort Packet.'

SIXTEEN

The widow Inge was the kind of woman a man might become obsessed about. Utah Bill Slaughter squeezed a hold on his feelings to keep from getting consumed by her quiet purity. She kept the one-room cabin tidy as a nunnery. Mementos from her home country were neatly placed around the room – a girlhood doll, a hand mirror that once belonged to her mother, Sven's pocket watch, a small ivory inlaid treasure box. She did not walk she glided, head high, shoulders back, blonde hair down to her lower spine, a small classical face, a fit, slim, perfect frame. She spoke little English. She was twenty-eight and Utah Bill knew she despised every breath of air he sucked in. His clumsy presence in her neat little cabin offended her. When he put his hands on her, she shriveled. That never stopped him because of the compulsion he had to own her. He wanted her submissive to every fantasy he had about her.

Utah Bill knew that one night or morning she might try to kill him.

When Red back-shot the deputy Lucas, Utah made sure he was in the cabin with Inge. He had already finished his business with Mr Blue and gave that alibi to Red. Utah had wanted to kill Lucas himself, but there would always be

Dode Lawson, the other shotgun-toter walking in the shadow of the marshal. He was older and had been around more than Lucas. He also had an obvious hankering for the good-looking widow marshal. No order had to come from Mr Blackwell to get rid of the deputies. Utah and Red figured it out. Blackwell wanted nobody in his way. He intended to marry up with the widow next month and lay claim to everything on her land.

Lying in bed with Inge, Utah worked his thoughts away from the pleasure that had just happened between them and shifted his thinking to how he might get a wagon load or two of that rich vein of silver. If he had any real sand, he'd get the property itself, find some way for the widow to give it up. He saw no need to marry it. Twist her arm and slap her around and make her sign the deed over. She had nobody in town to come to her rescue, no kin, no man friend, nobody except cow-eyed Dode who thought she walked on clouds. Mr Blackwell had other reasons to marry Rebecca Rogers besides the land. Maybe it was how she filled her dress or those tight buckskin pants she wore, or that she had too gentle a nature for the demands of being a town marshal – or many other reasons why a man looks at a woman and wants her.

It could be Blackwell really did want a woman at the ranch to keep it neat and clean, and fix meals and see to his personal needs. And help with Dougie, who was headed down a tumbleweed trail of destruction, either by getting himself killed in a draw he couldn't handle or putting Libby in a family way and living the rest of his life with that.

One thing Utah knew for certain. That other gun-fighter, Cort Packet had done his business and would be leaving town anytime. Thank God and that chestnut of his he'd be gone. Utah did not care for the competition. After what the gunfighter did to poor Yucca Frazel, Utah wasn't sure he wanted to tangle with the hombre. The man hated everybody and was as mean as a barrel full of rattlers.

Utah leaned over and gave Inge a good-night kiss. He blew out the lamp and settled down for sleep. He was used to her silence. He had told her she would not survive without him. She did not have the strength to shoe horses, nor speak English well enough for customers to board animals. She had her little garden and a few chickens, but nothing else. She had no answer for him. Nobody in town understood a word of Swedish. Like the marshal, and many young women who had lost their men, she was alone in this life. She had no income of her own, no skill, training, or education. Any money coming in had been from the black-smith, Sven, with a last name nobody could pronounce. Now, only Utah's generosity kept her out of the upstairs rooms of the Sip and Dip Saloon and Parlor House. Inge had stoically listened to the words without expression, then opened her Bible.

He stretched on his back with his hand high on her leg under the nightgown. His first sleep came troubled because he felt certain she did not like him much and she likely intended to someday do him harm.

That was why he felt only half-surprised when in early morning before dawn just before the moon went down, he saw a flash of reflection. He had been turned on his right side away from her. He felt movement on the bed and turned to his back reaching for the Colt on the nightstand. The flash came from the shiny blade of a butcher knife arcing down to him. Inge uttered something in Swedish he didn't understand. His left hand went up to clutch her wrist and block the blade but her plunge slipped by his hand. He pushed with his arm and felt slicing pain as the sharp edge cut his forearm. His right hand swung around holding the Colt. He hit her on the forehead with enough force to knock her off the bed. She sprawled on the floor and the knife skittered to the wood cook stove. He leaped off the bed after her.

When Inge pushed to her hands and knees, Utah kicked her in the stomach. He pushed the Peacemaker against her temple and cocked the hammer. She shut her eyes tight, waiting as if expecting the shot.

'No,' he said. 'Too easy. One bullet and all your troubles are over.' He stood straight and looked at his bleeding arm. 'You need to live with your troubles. No, little dove, you got to pay penance. If you were a man you'd have drawn your last breath, but you got a use. Not for me no more, but for other men. Slippery Sheila Calder will pay a pretty price for you, and that's where you're headed.'

Inge looked up at him, her lovely face twisted in hate. '*Ja*, you die. You need to die. *Ja*, you kill my Sven and I pray every night you will die soon, you filthy swine.'

It was almost noon when Utah put the pick aside because of the pain in his bandaged forearm and looked down the hill at Dougie, Dougie with his Peacemaker in his hand now practising the hip draw. Utah loaded the canvas with ore and slid it to the waiting gray mule below. The sun made him sweat. The mule was almost fully packed now. He felt irritated. His slick black clothes were dusted with dirt and stuck to his body. Dougie was useless as horns on a cat.

Dougie turned to him. 'How much you figure you got?'

Utah pulled his hat and wiped his brow. 'If you want any part of this, kid, you better replace that Colt in your hand with a pick handle.'

Dougie squinted and looked up the hill. He grinned at Utah. 'Naw, I'll get mine later when the sweet-faced marshal is my step-ma. Thinking on it, be nice to have her slinking

91

around the old ranch house in her unmentionables. Bet she has some good experience.'

'You better tone down the experience you're getting now.'

Dougie tilted his Montana Peak hat back and turned to look away from the hill. 'Yup, Libby has been kinda clingy lately. She even mentioned getting hitched. That ain't even in my poker hand. I'm too young to get hitched.'

'Might not be your choice.'

'Always my choice.' Dougie squinted off across the prairie and pulled down the brim of his hat to shield the sun. 'Rider on the mesa yonder.'

Utah looked in the direction Dougie pointed. A figure rode away from the edge of the mesa, too far to see clearly. It had been a man, dressed cowhand, sitting easy on his horse.

'Mebbe one of the ranch hands,' Utah said.

Dougie turned away and drew his Colt fast. 'Damn, this pard is fast. Come on, Utah. Stand here beside me. Let's see who's quickest.'

Utah worried his thinking about the stranger on the horse. A ranch hand might go running to Mr Blackwell, tell him about the Utah and Dougie, and the pack mule, and the picks. Wouldn't take long to figure it. Thievery going on and the gunfighter leading the son astray.

Utah had made a bargain with Mr Blue, Mr Blue no less greedy than other men would be with such a find. After fixing Mr Blue up with Dip and Sip's youngest and pretti-est, the assayer was eager for a deal that would give him a percentage of all silver pulled from the hill. A rider would be sent from Santa Fe to pick up the loaded pack mules after giving Utah his seventy-five per cent of the value.

Utah began packing picks and canvas sheets onto the mule. This was not the way to work the hill into a rich silver mine. The ore should be moved by a train of wagons, not pack mules, wagons one after another hauling tons not hundreds of pounds.

That would be impossible with Addison Blackwell lurking around. Utah looked over to Dougie. And the kid so eager to get himself shot down. They might both have to go.

'Come on,' Dougie said. 'Bet I'm faster. Stand beside me, Utah.'

Utah stared at the skinny kid. He knew that when he drew it would not be with Dougie standing beside him; it would be face-to-face, drawing against the cocky rabbit, giving the youngster his final practice lesson.

SEVENTEEN

Just past noon, Cort Packet rode Whiskey out of Scarlet. He'd had the nightmare again, seeing the Union young-sters die from his bullets, the one boy on his back coughing puke and blood over his face. Twelve years ago, and as vivid as the past ten minutes.

May was pushing on toward June and the land spread dry and light brown. Mesquite edges already started to change color into tumbleweeds. When Fall came, the harsh wind tore the weeds from their roots to roll across the prairie. Thin buffalo grass turned as sunburned and tan as the dirt holding it. In another month or so little green would be visible.

As Whiskey picked his way along the trail toward the Mescalero Apache reservation, Cort took time to think on his future. Life changes had sent him back to where he was eight years ago, living by the gun. He would take up bounty hunting again, maybe ease his way on down to the Tucson-Tombstone-Yuma area. He could even go back to Texas where plenty of bad hombres robbed and killed, enough to keep any bounty man busy. He might keep at it until a bullet claimed his vitals.

He would not be settling in Scarlet, though there was an enticement or two, and some clean-up yet be done there. More two-legged varmints sent into the ground. Might be it was the town and some of its twisted citizens that brought the nightmare back. Cort reckoned to deal with them before he left. And that brought to mind the image of Rebecca Rogers. Ah, the marshal and the picture of her teary grief over Lucas getting back-shot. That expression of loss on such a pretty face was enough to tug at a man's heart. If the heart could be tugged. And if the man had a heart.

The business with those who attacked him and his was over. All four of the jaspers were dead. But he felt no retribution, no sense of accomplishment, no real tie-off to it. Each had denied the act, lied about what they did as if that might be some kind of penance. If they did not admit the vile act, it must not have taken place. Cort knew it happened and who did it. The affair was done now. He only wished at least one of them had admitted the filthy deed.

Cort smelled the reservation before he came on it – cooking deer for the evening meal, dogs, horses, men, and the fires of burning juniper and mesquite. A breeze blew at him from the far end of a small canyon where the village sat. A quarter-mile away he saw smoke from tepees and huts rise up canyon walls to be snatched by wind and blown along toward him. Now he made out the first structure far in front, the adobe one-cabin headquarters for the Indian agent. The cabin squatted in the middle of the canyon separated from the tepees by a couple hundred yards of canyon floor and a chest high adobe wall.

A horse rode up from behind him, clomping along with no attempt at silence. Cort already had the Colt in his hand. He turned Whiskey to face the rider, the cowhand Jesse Ryan.

'Easy,' Ryan said as he reined to a stop. 'Easy, Cort. I ain't got no harm with me.'

Cort kept the Peacemaker aimed. 'What you dogging me for?'

'I lifted a few whiskey glasses one time or another with Newt Dugan. I can tell you some things about him you mebbe don't know.' His bright red kerchief outside the cowhide vest shined vivid in the afternoon sun. He pulled down the brim of his Montana Peak hat.

'Why?' Cort asked.

'He keeps a .44-.40 tucked in his belt, part hidden by his vest. He's older than his brother Charles, mebbe fifty. He's bald and fat. He has no neck and no face hair. A squaw-woman lives with him. Pretty little thing. More girl than woman. She ain't much more'n twenty, if that. Word is her family owes him or gets special treatment 'cause she's with him. He don't treat her so good. He's got a mean disposition and usually has one or two gun hands hanging about.'

Cort holstered the Colt. He turned Whiskey and walked the chestnut toward the adobe cabin. Jesse Ryan had his brown mustang fall in alongside.

Cort said, 'How does he work the beef?'

'You heard there's a shipment today.'

'From the marshal,' Cort said. 'Two wagons of goods. Tell me about the beef.'

Jesse looked around. 'How come the marshal ain't with you?'

Cort squinted ahead, beyond the adobe to the village. 'This is outside the marshal's territory. She's got something about the Sip and Dip. They got a new girl.'

'Yup, Inge, Sven's widow.'

Cort turned to watch Jesse's face. 'You been with her?'

'Nope. But Dougie has. I think he was her first customer. He'll pay hell when Libby finds out. He brags his pa give him unlimited credit. He'll be Inge's regular.'

'How come you ain't pushing Longhorns out at the Triangle-B?'

96

Jesse rubbed his stubble chin. 'I quit the Triangle-B. We buried Yucca and I got to thinking. The Triangle-B ain't no different from any other ranch I worked, and I worked more'n a dozen, a lot more. I ain't taking no more orders from Addison Blackwell or Utah Bill Slaughter, especially that runny-nose Dougie. They's some bad stuff going on, Cort, bad stuff. A lot worse than Newt cheating the Apache, though I know we're here to take care of that.'

That brought a smile from Cort. 'You figure to ride trail with me?'

'Mebbe for a spell. At least until we straighten what's crooked about Scarlet.'

'Could be the town ain't worth getting straight.'

'*She's* worth it, the marshal. I like her, Cort. I don't like old man Blackwell. Or Utah. Or the smart-alecky Dougie. And I don't like Charles and Newt Dugan. I reckon we'll be taking care of all them crooked bastards.' He nodded. 'We'll start with this here Indian agent, Newt Dugan.'

'Mebbe that's so, Jesse. You didn't tell me about the beef. How does the beef get to the village?'

'By wagon, slabs of it, wormy and slimy. Nobody knows how long it sets before they get it.'

'From the Triangle-B?'

'Yup. The old, the sick, them steers off their feed for one reason or another. They's butchered and sent along. Old Man Blackwell gets a pretty price for them too.'

Cort nodded. 'Besides being the biggest partner in the mercantile and swapping good government goods for rags and junk.'

Jesse sighed deep. 'Everybody doing it to the Apache on account of they's so easy. Fight gone right out of them. A defeated nation.'

'Not all of them. Not those down in the southwest. How come you care? Not many white folks do.'

Jesse was silent a spell. 'Had me a Shawnee squaw-woman once during my many trail rides. Ain't never knowed a gentler loving woman. I always walked tall in her eyes. When she looked at me I thought, damn, the woman might really like me. It was like mebbe I amounted to something, had some kinda stature to her. I knew better, but a man like me don't get that kind of feeling from women. She showed a lot more than like. She showed she loved me deep.' He pulled his Montana Peak and combed fingers through his thinning hair. When he returned the hat, he blinked hard against the sun. 'We rode and camped the prairies, the southwest, even down Mexico way for a time. Hunting and fishing for our needs. A bear got her up in Wyoming Territory. Clawed and chomped her to slivers. Like to shredded my heart with the loss. I killed and ate that bear, heart, liver and all. Cort, you ever hear of a woman makes a man feel better than he is? Just her by his side makes him want to be protective and good, even when it ain't his nature.'

'Yes,' Cort said. 'I knew one such woman.'

Jesse looked ahead as they walked their mounts. 'Anyways, that Shawnee woman made me look at the so-called savages from another angle.' Jesse reined in. 'Uh-oh, we got us some company.'

Five Apache braves rode toward them at a canter from the village. They wore buckskin and carried old '73 Winchesters.

Cort reined in with Jesse. The rawhide was off the hammer of his Colt. He got a grip on the Peacemaker, but kept it in the holster and waited. Jesse did the same. No hate or hostility showed in the eyes of the braves. No friendliness either.

When they reined up in front, the lead rider said, 'I am Long Arrow, Chief of this tribe. You are the Federal Marshal?'

Cort nodded a greeting. 'I am not. I am Cort Packet. I

come to deal with the cheating agent, Newt Dugan.'

Long Arrow had a thin face without expression and deep, dark intelligent eyes. Wrinkles pushed to the outside of his eyes, the only sign of his age, maybe in his forties. He looked at Cort's eyes as if taking a measure of the man. He looked at Jesse. His glance went to the adobe wall surrounding the agency, then to the cane next to the Winchester '76 on Cort's saddle. He squinted and sat straight on his pinto. 'Dugan is a federal agent. He is law from the government in Washington. He cannot be questioned. I have complained to the marshal about the beef and goods, to no good. Dugan tells us he is higher than the marshal, higher than Apache Chief. He is from the government and he can call in the cavalry if he is not obeyed. Bad men are around him, evil men with guns who insult our girls and women. The marshal tells us a federal marshal is coming. But she does nothing about Dugan. The summer will be hot and my young braves become restless. They talk the stupid war talk. They speak of leaving the reservation and joining Geronimo to the south. Why does the marshal not deal with the evil Dugan?'

Cort aimed his arm over the heads of the braves and swept it across the sky. 'The town marshal has no authority here.'

Long Arrow frowned puzzled. 'If the woman is without authority, what is to become of my village? The agent tells us he *is* the final authority. Nobody is higher. He speaks for the big chief of the white man. He does cheat us, but he is law and cannot be questioned.'

'So?' Cort said.

'If not the town marshal, who will stop the cheating? Who has authority over the Indian agent, Newt Dugan?'

'I do,' Cort Packet said.

EIGHTEEN

Newt Dugan appeared to be a busy man, a fat man wearing surplus Union army pants and a brown pullover no-collar wool shirt. Atop his bald head rested a black tattered derby. He had a sheet of paper in his hand as he walked around two modified Studebaker buckboards filled with clothes, blankets, pots, pans, picks, hoes, shovels and horse tack. Two men were on the wagons, one each on a driver seat. They were both dressed gambler dark. One carried two Remington pistols. The other had a single Colt Peacemaker. The holsters were tied down, the hammers looped. They wore flat-topped black hats.

Cort and Jesse rode to the hitching post at front of the open door and reined in. They dismounted and knotted the reins around the hitch. Cort kept the cane tied against his Winchester. He limped to the end of the hitch and leaned on it with his arms crossed. He felt his heart pounding. His forehead tingled with anticipation. He was not surprised. He had been like this before many times in many places before he was gentled by Amanda.

'Newt Dugan,' he said.

The wagon drivers looked at him with interest. They appeared to be almost thirty with lean smooth faces and thick black mustaches, like brothers, twins.

Jesse crossed in front of the open door and leaned back with the heel of one lopsided boot lifted against the wall.

Newt Dugan frowned at Cort. He swept the frown to Jesse.

A skinny young woman appeared in the doorway. She wore Apache buckskin with the skirt to her knees and moccasins to her calves. Her shiny black hair fell straight below her shoulders. Though she looked younger than twenty, her face held a musky, smoky expression too old for her years. Her manner showed she understood the situation. She was in the middle of something about to happen, a young Apache woman surrounded by white men.

Jesse turned his eyes to her. 'You best be staying inside, ma'am.'

The woman looked around the yard, at Dugan, the two gunslingers sitting on driver seats, the wagons, at Cort, then Jesse. 'Why? she asked.

Jesse said, 'No woman should look on what's about to happen.'

At the edge of the village closest to the adobe wall, Chief Long Arrow and his four braves sat their ponies and watched and waited. Their Winchesters rested in the crook of their arms.

Cort knew the braves had heard the words just spoken. They had been listening to all the words whites might come up with, words said by the white invaders since the time when their Indian ancestors rode and walked the land, words like so much noise in the wind. Now they sat on their ponies and watched to see if more stirred in the wind besides words.

Cort felt icy calmness flood his veins as it had many times before. He stood straight. 'You're a thief, Dugan, and it ends now.'

Jesse pushed away from the wall.

101

The Apache woman stayed in the doorway.

Dugan waddled two steps toward Cort. 'You make too much noise for a cripple. Who the hell do you think you are? More important, who do you think *I* am?' His small pale eyes sank into his fat face like marbles in a mud puddle. 'I'm in charge here.'

The two gunmen stood up in front of the wagon seats. They let the reins loose.

Cort said, 'I told you, it ends now.'

Dugan looked at the ground. 'Boys?'

'Take the left,' Cort said to Jesse.

Both men on the wagon drew at the same time. Cort already drew and had his Peacemaker out and shot the gunman on the right before the Colt cleared the man's holster. The one on the left fired toward Jesse before he was hit in the leg by Jesse's bullet. Cort aimed left and fired again as the first man tumbled over the wagon-wheel to the ground. The bullet hit the second man in the forehead. His head snapped back hard enough to throw off his hat. He fell backward off the wagon out of sight.

Newt Dugan reached under his vest and pulled his .44-.40. Jesse and Cort fired at the same time. Jesse's shot hit Dugan in the chest. Cort's pushed the nose into the fat face. Dugan arched toward the wagons and fell and rolled backward twice like a ball.

Without held reins, the four-up wagon horses reared and took off at a gallop out of the wall opening and away from the reservation, cargo rattling as loud as the gunshots. The four braves flanking Long Arrow heeled their ponies after the wagons, two on each. They rode to the front pair of horses and got the wagons stopped. In quick motions, they tied their ponies to the back and swung up to the driver seat. They pulled the four-up around to aim the wagons toward the reservation. They handled the reins clumsily, not knowing wagons.

Long Arrow did not ride after the wagons. He galloped his pinto hard toward the adobe wall. Cort and Jesse spun around when they heard the clump of the woman sitting hard in the doorway. Her hands clutched her bleeding stomach as she leaned back against the threshold, her eyes closed. The wild shot aimed at Jesse had found a mark. Once inside the wall, Long Arrow swung down and ran quickly to the fallen woman.

More people came from the reservation, walking and riding. Ten of them came to the yard in front of the door. Three women tended to the wounded girl, but she would not last long. Mostly, they could only murmur softly to her in Apache prayer. Long Arrow approached the girl. He knelt and placed his hand on her forehead and took her face in both his hands. He whispered something to her in Apache and touched his cheek to her forehead and moved away. He stood in front of Cort, the same height.

Cort said, 'I'm sorry, Long Arrow.'

Long Arrow showed tears. 'She was of no significance to the white eyes. But she was my daughter. Women will weep in their tepees tonight. Tears of grief would add to the hunger of their aching bellies.'

'We'll be doing something about them bellies,' Cort said. He limped toward Whiskey. 'Jesse?'

'Let's ride,' Jesse Ryan said.

On the trail an hour, riding west at a walk, Cort and Jesse pulled Bull Durham makings and lit up.

After blowing smoke, Jesse said, 'We been on Triangle-B land most of ten minutes now.'

Cort looked at the rich grassland around him. 'Where would the fattest steer graze?'

Jesse nodded to the north. 'Quarter mile out there.

Usually got a good-size herd. Got a stream running through a small valley.'

'We'll cut out ten and move them on down to the reservation. They been more than paid for.'

Jesse studied his cigarette while his mustang walked. 'Won't rotate the herd for another three weeks. We shouldn't run into any hands.'

'That was your job?'

'Part of my job. Me and Yucca worked together. Winters we was at line-shacks spreading hay so they wouldn't starve. In the spring we went higher up and brought down new calves and strays. Them dumb steers sure could wander off a far piece. Mostly, we rotated herds to new grazing ground. That's what the cowboy does, until spring branding.' He pulled another drag from his smoke. 'I miss old Yucca. A shame you had to put him down like that. Yup, he was ornery as me. We got in a few scrapes together, but he wasn't a bad sort of fella.'

Cort said, 'I'm sorry about Yucca, on account of he was your pard. But I had to bury the leavings of what them four jaspers done.'

Jesse squinted ahead, the cigarette stuck between his lips, deep wrinkles around his eyes. 'Yucca wouldn't have done such a thing. I lived with the man whole winters in a one-room shack. I knew him. We talked our lives to each other.' He stared off to the horizon. With one last drag on the smoke, he ground out the ember on his saddle and flipped it aside. 'Want you to think on something, Cort. Think real hard on it.'

'What?'

'What if them jaspers – Yucca and Ike and them other two – wasn't lying? What if they got drunk and used your house for a campfire out of cussed drunken meanness, and took your belongings, but didn't do the other? What if they

104

was telling the straight of it and it wasn't them? You think on that. If it wasn't them, who else could it have been done that terrible thing to your wife and boy? Who else was there?'

Cort felt the hair on the back of his neck bristle like a wind blew against it. He shivered despite the warmth. 'It *had* to have been them.'

'Uh-huh. Jest saying, pard. If not them, who?'

NINETEEN

Cort Packet found himself sitting on a bunk in a jail cell once again. He shared the cell with Jesse on the other bunk while Marshal Rebecca Rogers paced in front of her desk. Darkness had come and the lantern made her shadow move along the walls. The deputy Dode sat next to the door with the shotgun across his knees. His eyes never left Rebecca's form. She wore a fashionable dress with a tight waist and bodice, only her neck showing bare. Her shotgun rested on the desk. While Cort watched her bare neck, he pondered Jesse's words.

She stopped and spun to the cell. 'What were you thinking, Cort? You can't just ride out to the Indian agent and shoot him dead.'

'Him and his gunslingers drew first. It was a legal fight.'

'That's a fact, ma'am,' Jesse said. 'You can go talk to Long Arrow. Him and his village seen the whole thing.'

'Or you can take my word,' Cort said.

Rebecca stood in front of the cell. Her pretty face looked puzzled. She turned to Jesse. 'Can I trust you to bring him?'

Jesse swung to his feet. 'Yes'm. I'll go get him and he'll tell you the truth of it.'

Rebecca stood staring as if undecided. 'Charles Dugan

106

is livid with rage. He sent a store clerk to fetch Mr Blackwell.'

Cort jumped to his feet. 'Stop calling him, *Mr* Blackwell, Rebecca. He's a polecat that don't deserve that kind of respect from you. Him and the other Dugan brother are next.'

'Cort, I told you not to go on a rampage. You can't go around killing people.'

'I considered your words long and hard, then I reckoned some varmints just need killing.'

Rebecca unlocked the cell door. She stood aside as Jesse walked through. He strapped on his holster and exchanged glances with Cort. Cort had also noticed that Rebecca left the cell door open.

Jesse went out the door. The pound of horse hoofs faded away.

Dode stood. He fingered his pork chop whiskers. 'Time for the rounds.'

Rebecca frowned at him. 'Can you wait a couple hours? I'll come with you.'

Dode put his hand on her shoulder. 'It'll be fine, Marshal. I'll watch my own back. I'll keep in front of walls so nobody can sneak up on me. It ain't like I never been here before.'

'Be careful.' She watched him check the shotgun and his two Remington pistols. He closed the door behind him when he left.

Rebecca returned to her desk chair and sat heavily, a woman with obviously much on her mind.

'What about Inge?' Cort asked. His thinking felt cluttered, something he could not afford. He forced his gaze away from the arc of her smooth bare neck. Jesse's words crowded his head. He limped out of the cell and sat across from her.

'Take your gun belt, Cort,' she said. 'I don't know about Inge. I wish there was a way for her. Maybe she can sell the stable and find something else to get her out of that place. She seems to just accept whatever life deals her.' Rebecca sighed. 'I suppose there are women like that. Isn't that what we women have to do?'

Cort stood and buckled his gun belt. When he sat again he pulled the Peacemaker and checked the load. 'I ain't no expert on women and their plight.'

'No men are. Most men use women for their needs, like property. I know change will come. Already women have the vote in parts of Wyoming Territory. There've been some isolated strong ladies who made men notice. A few did it without becoming as noisy as men. I know change is coming as each generation of my sisters get stronger. It just won't happen in my time. My time is like my mother's.'

'You're a town marshal, Rebecca. Ain't many of your sisters can say that.'

'Arranged by a man who wanted to use me.' Rebecca stared at him. 'You must tell me. Why, Cort? What horrible thing did those men do to you to make you gun them down like that?'

Cort looked straight at her. 'They raped and murdered my wife. They bashed in my son's skull. I killed two at my place and hunted the other two. I got them, only now I don't know. Ike Jeffords and Yucca Frazel denied doing what they done. I know they done it. But they denied it on their dying breath. And Jesse has pushed doubt into me. Doubt I don't need to have. I can figure only one other way it could twist. If that's so, my killing ain't done.'

'Could be your killing isn't done here, either. I'm not thinking of citizens and store owners. Utah Bill Slaughter has to be dealt with. I can do it with my shotgun. But he's a special breed that needs a special way to die.'

Cort nodded. 'His turn in the barrel is coming, don't you worry about that, missy.'

A stretch of silence pushed between them.

Rebecca said, 'Don't call me missy. Addison calls me Becky and you call me missy. I don't like either. You men got to quit getting familiar just because it feels right to you.'

'I apologize. We all got parts of our life we don't like.'

'Yes. I'm told I will be a bride in three weeks. I'm to be part of a wedding ceremony I had no part in planning, and don't want.'

Cort returned the Colt to its holster. 'That won't happen unless you let it.'

'I got the same few weeks and I'm done with marshalling. And look what I got. Inge is working in that house. I got to find some kind of income for her out of it. The doc now says he's not sure what he saw when my husband was gunned down last year. Utah Bill Slaughter pressured him. I don't know how I can change his thinking to what really happened. Sven is gone and so is his testimony. The man who intends to take me as his wife is involved in the mercantile with Charles Dugan to keep cheating the Apache.' She leaned forward to look hard at Cort. 'You may have solved part of that.' She leaned back. 'Addison Blackwell is a bully. He's trying to bully me.'

'Only if you allow it, Rebecca. I keep telling you that.'

She patted the shotgun on the desk. 'I could do it your way I suppose.'

'Or I can do it.'

She shook her head. 'No, Cort. You've already done enough.' She tightened her lips. 'Except for Utah Bill Slaughter, who among other things, like the death of my husband, had something to do with the back-shooting of Lucas.' Her voice broke. She paused a moment. 'Slaughter pushed poor Inge to the Sip and Dip Saloon and Parlor House. Already her most frequent customer is Dougie Blackwell. Of course, Libby knows and is beside herself with worry.'

Cort said, 'Might be on account of Dougie left something in her belly?'

Rebecca turned to stare out the office window. 'Only she isn't sure it's his. Seems there was a drummer come through on the stage, a young man selling corsets and women's garments. And himself. And it may not even be him.' Rebecca shook her head. 'Libby likes attention. But she wants to be part of the Triangle-B. That's her life ambition.'

Cort pulled the makings of a smoke. 'And then there's you.'

Rebecca nodded. She looked steadily at Cort. 'Yes, me. And what about me, Cort?'

Cort rolled the paper around the tobacco and fired it from a match on the desk. 'I reckon mebbe this town ain't worth saving. I'm thinking mebbe you ought to move on, mebbe on up to Wyoming Territory where women got the vote.'

'Don't mock me, Cort.'

'No, ma'am.'

Rebecca leaned back in her chair. 'How would I do that? With what? If it cost a nickel to sail around the world, I couldn't get past the Scarlet town limit. I have no money saved. I don't even own a buggy or wagon.' She leaned forward with both hands spread on the desk, her pretty face serious and worried. 'Cort, I'm thirty years old with no husband and no children and no home and a job dominated by men telling me what to do, men too crooked for me to cope with. I own ten acres of land too barren to run cattle, too dry for a well, too rocky to plant crops, and with a cabin barely past the framing stage. Everybody I know is afraid of Addison Blackwell and he intends to take me as his bride. That is one path open to me. Be his wife and tend to his needs. I could do worse. I could be marshal for another year.'

'Your deputy worships you. He'd take care of you, if that's what you want, to be taken care of.'

'Dode is sweet. And I'd sure consider him before Addison. But Dode still grieves over his lost family and everything defeated during the war. No living woman can compete with a loving dead one. I'd never have his full attention.'

'It's another path.'

'Yes. Addison might want me to have his child. I want a child. But not his. And yet, that is the one realistic path open to me.'

'That's dumb talk,' Cort said. He inhaled and blew smoke at the ceiling. 'You think you'd be the only woman to cut and run with nothing?'

'I might do it if I had somebody with me. I wouldn't go the way Inge went. I just couldn't.'

'No need. No need for you. No need for her.'

Rebecca leaned back. She flicked her short brown hair with a toss of her head and looked straight at Cort's eyes. 'You got any interest in me at all, Cort Packet?'

'Not yet,' Cort Packet said.

TWENTY

With Addison Blackwell huffing and blustering in town, Jesse allowed as how it might be a good time for Cort and him to take a ride on out to the plains and said so to Cort. Jesse had something he wanted to show Cort. They rode slowly in the dark and in silence until they no longer saw town lights.

After two hours, Jesse said, 'We can set up camp here.'

They chose a rocky spot next to a sparkling gurgling moonlit creek, and after brushing enough rocks away to spread their blankets, Jesse got Arbuckle coffee boiling. He had some jerky and smoked ham which they ate and reduced by half. Coyotes were noisy, yapping off to the west. Cort spiked their cups with dollops of whiskey from his saddle-bags. They stretched, leaning against their saddles next to a mesquite fire and rolled smokes, the fire like a tiny flicker within the vast darkness beyond.

'You know this place,' Cort said. 'You been here.'

Jesse swept his arm out. 'Tomorrow, we'll ride onto the marshal's land. That there creek ain't got enough flow to cover a man's boot toe, and it dries up come about July. I got something for you to see.' He let a pause allow burning mesquite to crack loud for them. 'What you going to do about the marshal? She's partial to you.'

Cort took a drag and blew smoke at the fire. 'I got nothing inside me she can use. There ain't nothing kind about me.'

'Then you won't make a move on her?'

'Not at this time.'

'You'll let her marry up with Blackwell?'

'I didn't say that.'

'How will you stop it?'

'I'm betting she's got more sense. If not, mebbe I can postpone it with a few burials. Or, if she goes through with it, she might be a widow again real sudden.'

'You ain't letting that old man put his hands on her, are you?'

'She ain't the big problem in his life. Cheating the Apache is his biggest trouble. That, and hiding Red Jack Wheat on the ranch. If Red comes to town, I'll kill him. And Blackwell will have to go because there ain't no way he didn't know about Red shadow-shooting the marshal's husband or back-shooting the deputy, Lucas. Blackwell knew. Ain't no possible way he'll see a marriage bed with Rebecca Rogers, no matter how bad off she thinks she is.'

Jesse blew smoke to the blackness above him. 'She ain't as bad off as she thinks.'

'I'm hoping she'll use her wits and the good sense God give her.'

'But you ain't going to ease her out of the situation. You ain't taking part in her life.'

Cort sipped from his cup. 'No more'n I just told you. Not as big a part as she may like. A man lives with his memories. He can't just shut them out. It takes time. You know I got to clean up the mess now, got to get this done on account of I'll be leaving soon.'

Jesse took another drag. 'And then there is Utah Bill Slaughter.'

113

'He's a stump blocking the trail and has to be cut down. You know that. I know that. Utah knows that.'

Jesse flipped his cigarette into the fire. 'You thought on what I told you before, about your wife and boy?'

'I did.'

'And you think it may all warp another way.'

'I do.'

'Who else was there?'

Cort leaned his arm back on the saddle. He took a final drag and lobbed his cigarette to the fire and finished off the cup. 'My brother-in-law was there. Ned Perry. He may have ridden in soon as I lit out after that one-eyed milk cow, Butter. He could have even busted the gate so she'd wander off. He had all morning, past noon. If Amanda and Billy-Boy run from him, he'd catch the boy first, the boy only seven and slower. But Amanda wouldn't leave the boy, she'd keep him by her side. She wouldn't run off from him unless she knew he was dead. Perry would pistol whip the boy then go after Amanda. He'd have to hit her with something since he's a small puny critter as a man, and she might have whupped him. Mebbe a tree branch I didn't find. I'll look for it when I get back. Ned had scratches on his face I thought happened when his leg got shot and he fell from his horse against that juniper. I now reckon Amanda done his face fighting him off. He had beaten the boy, but he wanted Amanda intact and pretty when he did his business.' Cort coughed a little, found it hard to swallow. 'My boy.' His voice broke. 'I can still see his curly brown hair. He was only seven. And Amanda—' He looked away from the fire into the darkness.

Jesse still sat cross-legged. 'Are you sure about it, Cort?'

Cort lay back and stared at the billions of stars above him. 'Why was Ned there? He says he come to bring my fixed wagon axle he picked up from Santa Fe, only he don't have the axle with him. How come he didn't bring his wagon with the axle in it? He come alone on his horse. We wasn't friends enough for him to ride two hours just hungry for whiskey, spit, smoke and talk. No, he was there for one reason. His wife, Martha accused him of looking at Amanda with lust in his eyes. I heard her and it didn't sink in my thick head. She was so pretty, most men looked at her that way so I never figured beyond that. He had lust in his heart, likely lay awake nights thinking on how it would be when it happened. Dreamed about her and lived the events over and over. And it happened. And it was him. I never should have killed them four jaspers for burning a house and riding off with a few trinkets. They's worth beating a man senseless, mebbe crippling him, but them things ain't worth the killing. I done wrong and I know it now, and I got to live the rest of my life with the knowing. I got to make it right, as right as I can for Amanda and my boy. I already told you I was sorry about Yucca.'

Jesse tossed the rest of the liquid from his cup. 'Just ride in and gun him down?'

'No. I'll take the measure of him. That'll be about a minute. I'll look hard at his eyes and I'll know. Mebbe he confessed it to Martha, but I don't think so. She ain't the kind of wife to hold all her husband's confidence so he'd tell her everything. She'd look for nuggets of information in the confession to use, to get back at him, to lessen him as a man. He'd live bad with horror of how he left Amanda, but deep in his head he'd remember how it was just before, how good she felt and how much he liked it. He wouldn't share that remembered feeling with Martha or anyone else. That'd be his secret and it will get him killed. I'll take his measure then I'll know, and if it's so I'll shoot him down like a rabid wolf. If Martha gets in the way, I'll cut her down too. I'll burn their place and leave them for the prairie critters. All their stock will go to the reservation. Mostly mine anyway.'

Cort had the nightmare again, finding the extra Remington .44 and shooting the six Yankee soldiers, two running away, killing the remaining youngsters. The youngest on his back, heart-stopping scared, vomit bubbling out of his mouth mixed with the blood on his face from the shot while his body shook. Cort leaning against the hot barrel staring, unable to stand on his shattered leg. Cort jerked awake to daylight looking around.

Jesse sat watching Cort's sweating face. 'You don't sleep so good.'

'Haven't since the war.'

'Anything you want to talk on?'

'No.'

'We'll have coffee and the rest of that smoked ham. Then we got someplace to ride.'

As they broke camp, the sun brought warmth and was bright without a filtering cloud. A linen of light tan spread around them as Jesse rode ahead to lead the way. Sun-whitened rocks of all sizes dimpled the smooth ground crisscrossed with a weave of pale bronze prairie grass. Steep sandstone bluffs and mesas rose while off to the left stirrup-high cactus surrounded clumps of juniper and mesquite. The landscape contrasted with the bleached blue sky and a glaring silver sun.

Jesse led the way to a mesa not too steep to ride. The horses worked up with effort along a shallow trail already set. Atop the mesa, they swung down from saddles and walked to the western edge.

'Out there,' Jesse said. 'Up to the north, you can see the frame for the cabin.'

Cort looked to where Jesse pointed. 'This is Rebecca's

land, then.'

'It is. Look at that hill straight out from us. You see it's been scarred some, hacked into by men with picks and shovels.'

Cort stared. 'Looking for something.'

'And they found it. I followed them and come up on this mesa when they went to digging. I think they seen me but I watched them amble out with a pack mule loaded in ore.'

Cort turned to Jesse. 'Mr Blue come to town for a reason. He stayed out at the Triangle-B. The upcoming marriage is for a lot more than love and lust.'

Jesse took off his hat and wiped his brow with his forearm. 'Them wedding bells got a thud to their noise.'

Cort said. 'Was it Blackwell out here?'

Jesse put his hat back on and scratched his chin. 'The big man wouldn't lower himself. It was the gunfighter Utah Bill Slaughter and the spoiled kid. Mebbe the old man didn't even know they was here. Mebbe the gunfighter is trying to pull one over on him and got Dougie to throw in. I got to say, the kid didn't do any digging, jest practised his draw. I also got to say that was the hardest I ever seen Utah work. So that makes me think the gunfighter is in this for hisself. On down the trail, he'll get rid of the kid. Mebbe the old man too.'

'What did Mr Blue have to say?'

'He's a henpecked husband without much to prop him as a man. Get a few belly-burning belts of Sip and Dip con-coction down his throat and he tends to babble like that creek we just left. Have one of the prettiest youngest whores show him real attention and admiration he likely never gets at home and he'll tell her and a fella everything he knows.'

'Like what?'

'Like a deal he got worked out with Utah about the

117

richest vein of silver found within hundreds of miles.'

'Without Blackwell.'

'Yup. And you know what would send Blackwell's big plans for the marshal over a cliff like a stagecoach and turn it to kindling?'

Cort squatted to give some relief to his leg. 'If the marshal knew.'

'You got it, pard.'

TWENTY-ONE

At the burial of her deputy Lucas Price, Marshal Rebecca Rogers was aware who had shown up and who was absent. Most town merchants were there, Doc O'Connor, the banker, café operator and cook, the hotel owner, Albert Crutz, even some of the smaller ranchers. Dode, of course. Jesse Ryan and Cort Packet were there. A ride-through preacher spoke the words, a stranger to everybody present. The town of Scarlet had no church. Absent were Charles Dugan, his daughter Libby, Addison Blackwell, his son Dougie, and the gunman Utah Bill Slaughter. Nobody expected the Triangle-B foreman Red Jack Wheat to show. Somebody had to keep the spread operating, and he was hiding from questions.

A second burial was scheduled for early evening. Two on the same day because the preacher had to be riding on. That service was for the Indian agent, Newt Dugan, arranged for by his brother Charles. Nobody from the government would be there. Regrets had been sent by telegraph. Not enough notice. There would not be much of a turn-out because few actually liked the rotund agent. Red Jack Wheat was expected to ride in for that service. Those missing for Lucas would be there for Newt Dugan.

Rebecca had three days left as marshal. Elections came

next week. Several asked if she was running again. She emphatically told everyone, no. The mercantile owner Charles Dugan had thrown his hat in the ring. Word going around said he had the nod and backing of the big ranch owner Addison Blackwell. Blackwell told anyone who would listen that the current marshal would be taking up new duties, as a wife and stepmother. Interest had started months ago to get Doc O'Connor to run against Dugan. He showed no interest. However, in a fit of courage he had rewritten his statement about what he saw a year ago on the dark main road of Scarlet, across from the stables. He admitted he saw Red Jack Wheat, hidden in shadows, fire the first shot into Marshal Alfred Rogers, just before Utah drew and fired. The marshal had been hit twice before he cleared his holster.

Rebecca told Dode to run as marshal against Charles Dugan. He was more qualified and had a much better character. He said he would. For her. She mentioned that she didn't know his last name. He told her his name was Dode Lawson.

If Rebecca accomplished nothing else in the next few days, she intended to arrest Wheat for back-shooting Lucas, and especially for killing her husband last year. She stood in hot sunshine under the shade of her parasol listening to the preacher and thought of many things. She had already made her peace with the loss of Lucas. She did not care for the words at burials. Decisions had to be made and she had made them.

She felt she had been too timid to be marshal and was not good at it. The job accomplished what she was after. She now had the truth of how her husband died. And thanks to the gunfighter Cort Packet, the Apache would no longer be cheated by the agent. Who could know what lay in the future for the Apache? Another Indian agent? More stealing and cheating? She sighed as the preacher's words droned on. There would certainly be no wedding. Addison Blackwell had to choke that down as fact. If he attempted to force her, he would marry her shotgun. She intended to use Dode as backup and ride to the ranch if necessary to arrest Red Jack Wheat. If Wheat came in town for Newt Dugan's burial, the arrest would take place then. She would act as judge at the trial and the hanging would take place her last day in office. Addison might try to influence the jury with his power, in which case he would be arrested. If at any time during the process Wheat gave any resistance, she intended to cave in his chest with buckshot. Maybe she was not as timid as she – and others – had thought.

She wished she had Cort Packet as another-deputy.

She wouldn't mind having Cort for a few other things too. What she knew as certain as the rising of the sun, the day after her last marshal duty she was getting out of Scarlet and as far as her horse would take her. She had no money, no wagon for her meager possessions, no real destination or means to pay her way. But gone she would be. If Cort wanted her, she would give herself to him, anywhere he chose except Scarlet. But he showed no interest. She was not going to set herself up for heartbreak. Apparently, Cort had the same issues as Dode, lingering grief over lost love. No living woman could compete, nor would want to.

With the burial services done. Scarlet citizens clustered in groups of three and four to talk. Rebecca wanted to contact Albert Crutz the hotel owner and finalize what they had discussed yesterday. She went to him and waited for him to finish the conversation with the banker.

Albert Crutz overdressed for Scarlet. Most wore their best for a burial, but he looked like that all the time. Tall and thin, he always wore a tie with his blue suit and topped with a spotless black derby. His black boots were shiny. He never had a wife and Rebecca thought he looked and acted a little feminine. No question he was successful, as he owned the hotel outright.

Rebecca said, 'Mr Crutz, did you give any more thought to our discussion?'

He looked in his late forties and wore spectacles. 'I have. In fact, I was just talking financing.' He smiled. 'You look sparkling bright this afternoon, Marshal.'

'Thank you, sir.'

'The paperwork has been drawn up. If Inge will meet us at the bank tomorrow morning at nine, we can finalize the transfer.' He had full lips that he tightened. 'I think I may already have a blacksmith. Operating a stable will be much different than a hotel. Perhaps a better class of boarders.' He touched the front rim of his derby with his index finger. 'I apologize, Marshal. A crude remark.'

Rebecca asked, 'Can Inge stay in the cabin until the blacksmith gets here? I got to get her out of that place.'

'Of course. Should the blacksmith come, it won't be until the first of next month. What is she going to do with all that money?'

'Travel, I think.' Rebecca saw Jesse Ryan and Cort approach. 'Maybe go home to Sweden. Or maybe not.'

Walking up to her, Jesse said, 'Marshal? We got something you ought to know. It's important.'

Rebecca frowned from one to the other. 'Let's go to my office. But later. Right now, I want you two to do something for me.'

'Name it,' Cort said.

'Get to the Sip and Dip and yank Inge out of that brothel. I'll be waiting for her at the stable cabin.'

'Done,' Cort said.

*

As town folks drifted away from the graveyard up the hill behind the stables, Rebecca saw Dougie Blackwell enter the Sip and Dip. She hoped he didn't plan on a visit with Inge. Rebecca kept in the shadow of the parasol while she walked to the cabin behind the stable. Inge kept the key under a cactus plant by the porch. The covered porch only stretched in front of the cabin. Fifteen yards beyond was the corral then the stable for six horses, and in front of that, the blacksmith shop. Rebecca was at the door with the key in her hand when she felt rather than saw Addison Blackwell come up behind her.

'Rebecca, I'm sorry about Lucas.'

His hand touched her shoulder then moved down her back to her waist, a familiar gesture that offended her. She turned as she pushed his hand away. 'Addison, I want you to stop telling people about a wedding.' She faced him, a full head shorter and feeling much more fragile.

His creased face clouded as he stared down at her. He reached out to put his hand on her neck only to have it brushed away. 'You seem to forget your position, Becky.'

She backed until she felt the door against her. 'Stop thinking you can be close and touching with me. We're not close. What you're close to is getting arrested for what you and Charles Dugan are up to.'

He tried to step even nearer, to push against her. 'I know you're upset about Lucas, Becky, but this is silly talk. Your future is already laid out.'

'Yes, it is.' She placed her left hand on his chest and pushed him back a step. She rolled the parasol and held it across her chest close like a spear. She wished she had her shotgun. 'Soon as I clean out a few outlaws, I'm leaving the dust of Scarlet behind.'

The wrinkles of his brow deepened in a frown. 'No, you're not, young lady. You're going to be part of the

Triangle-B. Damn it, Becky, I need you.'

'What you need from a woman is available at the Sip and Dip brothel. I want you to deliver the murdering Red Jack Wheat to me at my office.'

'What?' He stood straight and took a step back. 'I have the buggy. We're going to the ranch, now.'

Rebecca's heartbeat had been racing. She held the parasol fully prepared to stick him through the stomach. She had been bluffing at being brave. But she would not be getting in any buggy. She had to continue. 'You are so full of yourself few outside words reach you. Get this straight in your arrogant head. No wedding. No ranch. No wife and stepmother. Not with me. Not the longest day you live.'

He reached out to circle her waist. 'We'll just see about that.'

Behind him, she saw Dode walk up to the porch. 'Marshal, is this old man bothering you?' Dode had his shotgun aimed at Blackwell's back.

TWENTY-TWO

Slippery Sheila Calder kept shaking her big head at Cort and Jesse. 'You ain't doing nothing of the kind. Inge is becoming my most popular gal and you ain't taking her no place. I bought and paid Yankee gold for her. She belongs to me.'

Cort glanced around looking for Sheila's backup. She usually had a few guns on her payroll. 'We come to you as a courtesy. It wasn't necessary. Any gold problems you got, take up with Utah Bill Slaughter. Inge wasn't his to sell. Damn it, woman, a war was fought so that didn't happen no more. You don't buy and sell people.'

'Get your head out of the water bucket, gunfighter. In the real world people been bought and sold since Bible days and especially Bible nights. It ain't never stopped and never will. Don't interfere with commerce.'

'I ain't. Just so you're clear, Inge is leaving, *now.*'

Cort followed Jesse along the balcony to Inge's room. The rooms were busy what with men stuck between burials, and the preacher downstairs lifting a few with merchants. When they reached the room, Cort turned to see Slippery Sheila talk with two rough-looking drifters and nod to him. The drifters turned away from her and stomped along the balcony toward him.

The door to Inge's room was closed but not locked. Without hesitation, Jesse shoved it open and pushed inside, Cort right behind. A man was in the room with

Inge, on top of her in the bed making guttural noises and breathing hard. His pants were bunched around his ankles. He still had his dusty boots and dirty shirt on. His tattered Stetson was on the back of his head. Cort stood at the open doorway looking back along the balcony walkway.

Jesse grabbed the lover by his collar and yanked him off Inge. 'You're done, jasper.'

The man was a boy not yet twenty. He flailed his arms and went to the floor. He scrambled on his knees to the chair where his holster draped. 'I paid my three dollars for a poke and by God, I'll get my poke.'

'With somebody else,' Jesse said. He swung his pistol against the young head and grabbed the shirt again. Before the young man could clear his holster at the chair, Jesse dragged and tossed him toward the door.

Cort helped the boy move on through where he bounced against the balcony rail and almost fell down the stairs, the whole time yanking and pulling up his pants.

Jesse picked up the holster and lobbed it empty out the door. 'You can pick up your hog leg in the street.' He tossed the Colt out the open window. When he turned back to the bed he touched the brim of his Montana Peak hat. 'Get yourself dressed, little lady. You're leaving this place.'

Inge had not moved. She had enough presence to pull a sheet over her. Most of her lipstick had been smeared off her lips. Blinking with confusion, she showed she did not have to hear the words twice. She pushed back the sheet and slid off the bed reaching for her dress.

Jesse stared openly.

Even Cort had to glance in. Not only was the woman beautiful, but he could see why she had become so popular. But Cort had other images to draw his attention. The two rough *hombres* marched along the balcony from Slippery Sheila close to Inge's room, clawing at their holsters.

Cort drew and fired, dropping the one on the left. The sound of the shot cracked around the ceiling upstairs and down. The *hombre* hugged his chest and tumbled over the waist-high balcony rail. He dropped on the piano to the screeching and the ping of musical notes. As Jesse came out of the room with the red of his kerchief bright, he drew his pistol. The second *hombre* fired a shot that made Cort duck. Cort returned two quick bullets that doubled the man and he stumbled two more steps and fell face down on the balcony floor.

By then Inge had her pretty pink shoes and her red dress on and came up behind Jesse. Jesse wrapped his left arm tightly around her tiny waist. Her long almost-white hair set off her angelic face.

'*Ja*,' Inge said.

'This way.' Cort led them to the stairs and down, the Peacemaker in his hand. Jesse followed holding Inge tight, sweeping his six-shooter back and forth across the crowd. At the noise of gunshots, the drinking crowd had paused to stare just long enough for another glass to be filled. They now watched the three come down.

Fuming at the other end of the balcony, Slippery Sheila shouted. 'Somebody shoot down them two kidnappers. Two five-dollar gold coins for anyone who does it.'

A gambler stepped out from the bar and pulled a cross-draw Remington.

Cort fired and the gambler bounced back against the bar and slid down bleeding from his left eye.

Cort looked up at her. 'You get my next bullet, Sheila. We're here on order from the marshal. Nobody gets in our way.'

A young man's voice spoke from just inside the open swinging doors. 'I'm next with Inge. I'll be getting in your way, Cort Packet. Holster your six-gun and we'll see who gives orders.'

Cort turned away from the bar crowd to look at the face of young Dougie Blackwell.

They were close to the doors, the doors still moving slightly on an incoming breeze. With his Colt aimed at Dougie, Cort put his hand on Jesse's shoulder. 'Take her on out.'

Inge clung to Jesse as he pulled her tighter and swept her through the doors and onto the boardwalk outside. When he released her, she still hung on to him as they crossed to the stables, her head on his chest, Jesse watching the street for hostile guns.

'You heard me, Cort Packet,' Dougie said. 'I am scary fast, as you'll soon find out. Holster your pistol and we'll see who draws quickest.'

Cort cocked the hammer of the Peacemaker. His thinking considered three shots fired, three left. Slippery Sheila stood with her pudgy hands on the balcony rail looking down at the saloon, her plump face scarlet, silent. Three soiled doves between gents had come out of their rooms and looked down at the scene. Those at the saloon bar remained still and stared. He had no intention of getting into a manhood contest with this blustery colt. 'Go home, boy. Live to see another sunrise.'

'Not 'til you're dead, gunfighter,' Dougie said.

Cort studied the blemished thin face, the big nose, the thin mouth, the eyes too close together showing a trace of genuine fear. He took a step closer and aimed for Dougie's forehead. 'You think you can draw before I blow your head apart?'

The boy squinted to push away the fear. He believed in himself and his ability, yet Cort reckoned a sensible part of him doubted both. 'You can take the coward way if you want, Cort Packet.'

Cort watched the eyes. What he saw caused his forehead

to tingle. His armpits and face began to sweat. The eyes were the same as the nightmare. *Behind the bravado, this boy saw his own death. It was as if he lay on a battlefield surrounded by thick smoke and fog and the sound of gunfire and felt blood ooze out from the bullet hole, his face soon covered with it. The boy had tasted it and lurched with vomit that mixed with the blood and spread over his face. He lurched again. Cort had sweated then, as he did now.* He had dreamt the nightmare over and over, almost every night. And here it was again, years later in a saloon instead of a battlefield. A different boy, but the same look in the eyes, the same unsure, not understanding look, the same bravado to push away the terror of dying. The young face in front of him carried the arrogance of his father, belief in his own ability, but not much substance to back it.

What to do next?

Cort took a deep breath. 'You don't die today, boy. Move away.'

The boy's thin mouth worked to a grin. 'You're afraid of me.'

He looked to the saloon bar. 'The old man has lost it. He knows I'll drop him like a blanket. He takes the coward way.' He leaned forward squinting at Cort. 'You hear what I said? I'm saying you're a coward. Holster your Colt and let's answer this.'

Cort pushed the Colt harder against Dougie's forehead. He yanked one pistol from the boy's holster and threw it out between the swinging doors. He pulled the other and did the same. The young eyes looked surprised, puzzled. Cort raised his Colt high and brought it down hard on the Montana Peak crushing it flat. When Dougie's shoulders slumped, Cort raked the Colt across his cheek. Before Dougie fell, Cort grabbed the front of his flowery shirt and smashed the butt against his nose. Dougie dropped like a poured bucket of whiskey.

TWENTY-THREE

Inside the cabin at the back of the stables, Inge splashed in her tub behind a double curtain. Marshal Rebecca Rogers sat in the comfortable armchair that had come from Sweden. Her pretty face showed she hung on Jesse's every word as she leaned with her elbows on her legs, her hands clutched at the knees as if she hid a ball of yarn. Her mouth was slightly open while she stared at him without a blink. Cort sat in a less comfortable chair rubbing his left leg, staying silent, letting Jesse run with it.

When Jesse had told her all of it, she leaned back in the chair. She looked at the curtain with Inge behind it. She looked at Cort. She turned back to Jesse. 'Are you sure? You mean all that silver is on my property?'

'Yes'm,' Jesse said.

'And you *saw* Utah Bill Slaughter and Dougie stealing it?'

'Yes'm.'

'But you don't know if Mr Blackwell is involved?'

'Marshal,' Cort said. 'I told you, quit giving that rat-tlesnake respect when he don't give you none at all.'

Jesse said, 'No ma'am, I don't. I do know Mr Blue, the assayer from Santa Fe, stayed at Triangle-B ranch. I reckon he figured the value of them samples Slaughter stole. Cort and me think the mule loads of ore they already took are to sell someplace. A man is in town who works for Mr Blue. Blackwell likely knows what's going on.'

The marshal turned back to Cort. 'You knew about this?'

'I did when Jesse showed me.'

'Did you see Slaughter take any of my silver?'

'No.'

Rebecca Rogers sat still in the chair and stared at the floor between her feet. She remained motionless for a full minute. She looked up at the curtain with splashing going on behind. She turned back to Jesse. 'They can't do that. The deed gives me all mineral rights to the property. Nobody can take samples or dig for ore except me. I'll be wanting a copy of that assay report.'

Jesse said, 'I reckon Blackwell has it.'

Rebecca drummed her fingers on the arm of the chair. She smiled at the curtain. 'Did you hear that, Inge?'

'*Ja,*' Inge said.

'I'm a rich woman.'

'*Ja.* Me too tomorrow morning.'

'Maybe two rich women ought to stick together some-place else.'

'Someplace else. I like that, *ja,*' Inge said.

Rebecca leaned back in the chair. She looked from Jesse to Cort. 'When Inge has herself clean, we'll make plans. A woman can do that, you know. No matter how men use and abuse her body, she can always wash herself clean. She can heal herself. She can come out of the tub a new woman. Inge will be a new woman. We decided to change her last name since hers is so hard to say. We can do that. Two independent rich women can do anything they like. She'll be Inge Sweden, a woman of means, when she sells this property,' Rebecca said, looking and sounding excited, running her words fast together.

131

Inge had stepped out of the tub and was now behind the curtain toweling herself dry.

Cort said, 'Marshal, you ought to be thinking on what you'll do as the law in this town. Blackwell has gone back to the ranch. Charles Dugan went with him. Dougie is with Doc O'Connor getting patched up.'

'Thanks to you,' Rebecca said.

'Yes'm.'

'He won't forget what you did to him.'

'No, ma'am.'

Rebecca sighed deeply. 'I asked you to take Inge out of that place. I didn't tell you to shoot the saloon to pieces.'

'Time and circumstance, Rebecca,' Cort said. He shook his head. 'I don't know what to call you, Rebecca or Marshal, without you going into a conniption fit. I ain't calling you Becky or Missy or I suffer your wrath.'

The corners of her mouth raised just a little. 'Rebecca will work just fine for you, Cort.'

'I got to tell you, Rebecca, I ain't staying around. I got to be someplace and I'll be moving on.'

Rebecca frowned. 'Someplace, where?'

'Someplace else. Since Blackwell is back home, I don't reckon Red Jack Wheat will be coming to town for no burial. Charles might because it's his brother's burial. You want Red you got to go out and get him.'

Rebecca leaned forward. 'Cort, Jesse, I intend to arrest Addison Blackwell for trespassing and stealing my silver. I'll be asking him about the Apache too. I'll be arresting Utah Bill Slaughter and Dougie. And the same with Red Jack Wheat for the murder of my husband and my deputy Lucas. I'm concerned about Libby. She's in a family way and yesterday she said she intended to tell Addison he was about to become a grandpa. And when would she be moving to the ranch? And when was the wedding between her and Dougie?'

'That ain't smart,' Jesse said, 'Libby talking to Blackwell being pushy and demanding.' He rose and tilted his hat back and looked at the curtain, and went to stand by the window.

Rebecca nodded. 'Too many weddings getting tossed around.'

Cort said, 'Blackwell will have to do something about Libby.'

Rebecca inhaled with her mouth slightly open and the frown deepened. 'Yes. I want you and Jesse with me and Dode.'

'Yes'm.'

'As deputies.'

From the window, without turning, Jesse said, 'That ain't the side of the fence I usually ride on.'

'Me neither,' Cort said.

Rebecca glanced from one to the other. 'I don't care. I won't stand for unlawful killing. If they put up a fight, I want you two as deputies. I'm certain it isn't the first time that's happened, questionable gun hands working for the law. I'll swear you in before we leave this cabin.'

Jesse still did not turn. 'I ain't wearing no badge. Sticks out like a target, all slick and shiny.'

'You have to take the badge. Don't wear it if that suits you.'

'Sticks in my craw,' Jesse said.

Rebecca turned to Cort. 'What will Blackwell do about Libby?'

'What has to be done.'

'He wouldn't do her harm, would he?'

'He's got to,' Cort said. He rubbed his leg. 'He don't strike me as a fella wants some bastard off-spring growing to take what he built. He'll have Slaughter or Red take care of it 'cause that's how he is.'

Rebecca stood. 'Well, there is nothing he can do from a jail cell. I'm arresting him.'

Cort stood towering over her. 'Don't be naive enough to think he'll go peaceably to any arrest. If he knows you're coming, he'll be waiting with men and guns. Anything to be done about Libby has already been done.'

'You don't know that.'

'Small town,' Jesse said from the window without turning. 'Folks talk. If Libby told the marshal about her condition, she told the doc. She'd have to. She was getting examined. She'd tell the doc, Dougie was the father, if he is or ain't. No way to know how many others heard. And since I reckon Dougie told her about the silver and how they'd be rich, she told that to the doc too. And who knows who else she told? And who the doc told when he had a snoot on? Red already guesses the marshal is going to arrest him or try to. Libby's daddy had been cheating the Apache with his brother. With Newt about to be planted out there close to Lucas, Blackwell and Charles will need another plan for the Apache. Soon as Blackstone hears demands from that snippet of a girl about her being with child and it being Dougie's he'll do something.' Jesse talked to the curtain, staring outside as if studying the main road. 'And when Blackstone sees what Cort done to his brat, he'll have a hog leg hanging on his hip. And guns around him. All of them would think the marshal was coming and had to be dealt with. I reckon Libby has already gone on to another place.'

'You don't know that, Jesse,' Rebecca said.

'Tell you what I do know, Marshal. Dougie just mounted up and rode on out of town, his face all bandaged and bright in the afternoon sun. Where you figure he's headed?'

TWENTY-FOUR

Cort Packet kept Whiskey next to the marshal's roan. They rode at an easy canter so the horses saved themselves for the distance. Rebecca wore her buckskin pants and linen shirt, and the overcoat that must have belonged to her Confederate daddy. Jesse stayed in the rear on his mustang next to Dode. Rebecca and Dode carried shotguns. Jesse and Cort kept to their sidearms, with Winchesters in their saddle scabbards.

Cort did not figure on much conversation. Nor did he think there would be any arrests. He gritted his teeth feeling an urgency. There were other places he needed to be.

Late afternoon brought light grey clouds, followed by black thunderheads moving overhead faster to take over. Jagged strips of lightning speared at mountain tops to the north above Raton Pass. They rode under the Triangle-B arch when the first drops fell. The rain came light at first, as if hesitant, dampening the way for the big dollops to follow.

Twenty minutes out from the ranch, they stopped to put on rain slickers. They remained silent. Cort figured each of them calculated how events would play out in the next hour or so. He knew nobody at the ranch would go peaceably. As they rode on, the rain came down in a steady hiss, splattering the plains that soaked up the moisture, the drops getting thicker and falling faster until the horses rode through sandy mud.

Through a curtain of rain, outbuildings became visible. Behind the ranch house and barn, a clump of boulders pushed up among cottonwood, firs and pines. They went about one hundred feet to a flat mesa. Beyond, the ragged land rose to meet hills and mountains.

Though mid-afternoon, lanterns lit the main window of the house. Shacks and buildings and outhouses sagged gray and shiny in mud puddles outside the ranch house. The bunkhouse had smoke coming from a Franklyn stove, and dark windows.

Cort said, 'Me and Jesse will ride out flank. You better get your shotguns in hand, ready.'

Cort went right, Jesse left. Cort rode out ten to fifteen yards then circled back to the side of the ranch house. Squinting, he saw Rebecca and Dode ride in, shotguns at the ready.

The first shot came from the bunkhouse, sounding muffled through the rain. Dode jerked to his left and fell from the saddle. Rebecca unloaded a roaring blast toward the building. A window shattered. A man Cort did not recognize came out the door from the bunkhouse. He wore no slicker and his cowboy outfit quickly soaked. He saw Jesse riding hard for him and fired his pistol. The shot missed and Jesse put two bullets into the man. He stumbled back against the wall and slid down.

Jesse shouted as he reined in his mustang, 'Red Jack Wheat, get your sorry ass out here. I aim to shoot you dead.'

Wheat slid sideways through the door and ran alongside the wall, hopping over the dead cowboy. He fired wild twice as he ran, headed for the corral and his horse. Jesse shot him in the leg, which caused him to tumble and bounce, but he held onto his pistol.

Jesse rode up to him. 'Is Libby still alive?'

By now, Rebecca was at the front of the ranch house. She dismounted and moved behind the water trough. 'Come out of there. Addison Blackwell, you're under arrest.'

From the bunkhouse, three cowboys sprinted out the back door to the corral where they mounted their saddled ponies and rode off for the boulder hills. Their silhouettes soon became lost in the pouring rain.

Cort saw this as he dismounted and approached the back door to the ranch house. He could just make out the horse trough. He did not think ordinary ranch hands wanted to buy into the noise about to take place. One of theirs was already down, the first man Jesse shot. The rest had other places to be. Ranch pay only covered so much. Two more hands joined them and rode off.

Red Jack Wheat mumbled something to Jesse and raised his pistol. Jesse shot him in the temple.

From the horse trough, Rebecca shouted, 'Blackwell, you and Dougie and Dugan and the gunfighter get your-selves on out here. I'm taking you all to jail.' Her voice sounded soft and weak in the roar of rain.

A shot came from the house that hit the trough and caused a pencil spurt just visible on the dimpled surface. Rebecca ducked and brought the shotgun to the top of the trough. Behind her, Jesse swung down from his mustang and knelt alongside.

Fifteen yards out, Dode started crawling toward the ranch house.

A short silence followed. Cort moved close to the back door, the Colt in his hand. He slid two steps along the wall from the side of the door and swung his Colt to smash the window. Two shots rang out, one chipping the sill. Cort ducked and shuffled under the window then raised himself enough to see through. He fired one shot that tore through Charles Dugan's left cheek. Three more shots came through the window. By then Cort was back at the door and had kicked it off its hinges. He ignored the pain in his left leg as he bent and hobbled inside the kitchen to the left. Another shot pinged off a hanging pot.

Addison Blackwell was toward the front of the ranch house. 'Becky, we can talk about this.'

'All right,' she shouted. 'Throw down your guns and come out.'

'It's pouring rain. You come in. Nobody will shoot you.'

From the kitchen, Cort saw Dougie slipping toward the back door, maybe to circle around the house and back-shoot Rebecca and Jesse. His facial bandages looked like a partial white mask.

Outside, Rebecca said, 'Where's Libby? I want to see she's not harmed.'

A shadow moved toward one of the back bedrooms to the side of the ranch house. The sound of a window slid open.

Cort immediately thought, Utah Bill Slaughter. He stepped from the kitchen shadow. 'Drop the hog leg, Dougie.'

Dougie jerked in surprise. He grinned which made his face look grotesque. 'I'll just put my Peacemakers here in their holsters. Turn to face me, gunfighter. Holster your Colt.'

'No.' Cort kept the Colt aimed at him. He waited for the nightmare he had felt in the saloon to return, the same that haunted him in his sleep night after night, the same that came back at the sight of the boy. The smoke and gunfire of the battlefield were there, but the two shot boys did not appear. He breathed deep watching Dougie. 'Tell me about Libby. You got her buried someplace?'

Dougie blinked. His bandaged face made him look like a cornered badger. 'You know what she tried to do? She braced my pa, tried to convince him the brat she carried was mine, *mine*, and her laying with every saddle-tramp come riding through. I ain't dumb, mister. I wanted Inge as my very own, even wanted to buy her. Was going to pay hard solid gold coin. Pa said it was OK. I could buy her and keep her, long as she stayed in the Sip and Dip, or her cabin at the stables. One night with Inge, I could never go back to that bounce-around Libby. She was like a silver dollar. You know? What them fellas say? A woman goes from man to man like a silver dollar goes from hand to hand. And I was first. I mean Libby told me I was first. Pa tells me females lie all the time. You know what I mean, gun hand?'

'You talk too much, Dougie. Who killed Libby? You or your pa?'

'Ha! Pa wouldn't let me. And *he* sure didn't do nothing like that.'

'Like what?'

'Pa give her to Utah so he could take her out to the barn. Pa says for Utah to do whatever he wanted with her, make fun with her. But be sure whatever noise she makes is her last. I reckon she's still out there. Ain't had time to bury her.' He looked down at the body by the window. 'Is that Charlie Dugan? You killed my pa's partner?'

'And I ain't done.'

Out front of the ranch, Rebecca shouted, 'I said to get yourself out here, Blackwell. There's been enough killing. Where is Libby Dugan?'

Cort could not see Blackwell. He held his Colt on Dougie. Dougie still stared at the body of Charles Dugan.

The rain became a waterfall pounding on the roof of the house, which brought a bone chill to the kitchen air.

Dougie nodded to the body. 'He never knew. He had no idea what happened to his little girl. We told him she never come out to the ranch and he accepted that. Dumb as a fence post.'

'Not smart like you and your pa,' Cort said.

'My pa ain't so smart. Me and Utah going to take that silver right away from him, and he don't know it.'

'The marshal knows.'

Dougie frowned. 'Knows what?'

'About the silver. She's selling the property to the hotel owner, Albert Crutz.'

'Get outta here.'

'You're done, Dougie. You and Slaughter ain't never going to see another sunrise.'

'Says who? Holster your hog leg, gun hand. I'll outdraw you and shoot you dead. I'm scary fast.'

From the living room, Addison Blackwell said, 'What the hell is going on out there?'

Outside, Rebecca shouted. 'Get rid of your weapons, Blackwell, we're coming in.'

Cort saw Blackwell's shadow move across to the front door, a pistol in each hand. Cort fired hitting Blackwell somewhere in the left arm. Dougie drew and shot too fast, the bullet hitting the oven door. Cort shot Dougie in the stomach then cocked and stepped forward to shoot him again in the side of the bandaged face. Dougie dropped to his knees. Cort moved behind the Montana Peak hat and fired a bullet into the top of his head. He did not see a boy lying by a field cannon vomiting puke and blood. He saw a poisoned mind and a low character taking after his pa, admiring a back-shooting gunfighter. He saw a young snake stealing from a troubled woman.

140

As the front door burst open, Jesse came in first, low and to the right. Cort had moved down the short hallway to the living room. Blackwell shot at the fast-moving Jesse, missed, then turned toward Cort. Rebecca came in with her shotgun, looking small, boyish, her dark slicker shiny. A roar exploded through the house as she unloaded her final barrel into Blackwell's neck severing most of his head. She watched him fall with wide eyes, frozen in her steps. Her mouth dropped open. Her chin began to shiver. She pushed the shotgun away onto his body as if the act ended everything for her.

'Enough!' she cried. 'I can't do any more of this.'

Cort had already turned back to the kitchen. 'Jesse, help her get Dode inside.'

'Libby?' Jesse asked.

'In the barn. Too late.'

'Cort?' Rebecca cried. 'Cort?'

'Slaughter,' was all Cort said as he hobbled toward the open back doorway and outside where Whiskey waited.

TWENTY-FIVE

Rain poured in steady sheets. Whiskey picked his way care-fully as Cort studied the wet ground. Horse prints left deep impressions in the mud and filled with water as if they were patterns for clay molds. The little-used trail went around boulders and between trees, some overgrowth in places, climbing toward the flat mesa. A rider would have to go around the mesa to reach foothills and mountains and escape. Rain flowed and dripped everywhere from every-thing, splashing through gulleys in places and creating small streams. The way proved slippery through the mud, but Whiskey was a good trail horse and stepped carefully. Cort did not push the chestnut but let him pick his steps.

Not so Slaughter, as mean a hombre as there could be to man and horse. A man looking for escape, if not scared then knowing bullets waited for him. A man knowing by now that to get away he would have to come down off the mesa by the same trail, then go around it to find moun-tains. A man now cursing himself for not taking the long way around the mesa. A town man, used saloons and parlors and midnight shadow gunfights and back-shooting, not used to open trail riding.

Cort never questioned he would come on the killer and gun him down. Killing Slaughter would put an end to his time in Scarlet. When he saw Slaughter's bay limp one step to him along the trail, he reined in Whiskey and frowned. A horse with a broken leg would stand, not walk down a muddy twisting trail. He could not have come far, a step or two. Maybe the bay remembered other horses, a corral, help at the bottom of the trail. Or he heard Whiskey coming and wanted to be seen. Who knew? Could be the bay had been standing a long time on that broken leg? More than an hour?

Cort knew he should put the animal out of its misery. The bay drooped in the rain, his head low, his broken left front leg lifted, empty saddle shiny wet. Each movement with the leg on the muddy slippery trail caused him to wheeze with the pain of suffering. He snorted to blow wet from his nostrils. As Cort approached, the bay looked at Whiskey, not Cort.

Cort reached out and took hold of the bay's reins. The bay panted and shook his head spraying water. He had been spurred hard along an uneven trail. Rain did not wash all the blood from the spur cuts along his sides. Whiskey stood still and silent. Cort pulled the reins, turning the bay toward him. Slaughter would hear the shot and know where Cort was. He would hide behind a tree or boulder, pistol in hand, ready to dry gulch Cort as he came by.

The bay snorted again, his nostrils close to the mud.

Cort pulled his Peacemaker. With the reins, he raised the bay's head and shot him through the left eye. The sound ricocheted off the mesa and the hills and mountains beyond and faded away in the rain. The bay stumbled one step and went down heavy. He slid less than a foot and lay still. Whiskey bucked slightly and shook his head.

'Settle yourself,' Cort said.

Cort looked through a waterfall curtain out along the muddy trail. It would become steeper and more twisty as it climbed higher. Until now, Slaughter likely wasn't sure anyone came after him. He had gotten out the bedroom window and away before the gunplay at the house was over. He sure knew now. And he knew exactly where Cort was. Maybe he thought he might turn back, ride down to the bottom again and go around toward the mountains. He not only needed Cort dead to make a clean escape; he needed Cort's horse.

Cort walked Whiskey to the next curve. Looking up he saw he was still twenty yards from the top of the mesa. Slaughter had made it. From what Cort could see, the mesa looked flat with clusters of growth, juniper and mesquite, a few isolated pines.

The rainfall began to lighten. Grimacing in pain, Cort swung down from the saddle and tied Whiskey to a pine. He limped off climbing, the way slow and slippery. An hour later when he reached the flat top, pain pounded in his leg. He had left his cane on the saddle. It would have been useless in this mud. From what he saw across the mesa, all sides dropped sheer, a fall of a hundred feet. The only trail in was the one Slaughter had taken. It was the only trail out. Cort had needed both hands and feet for the last fifteen yards so left the Colt holstered, the hammer looped.

The rain stopped but the sky remained dark with clouds. The sandstone mesa spread flat with puddles. Once on the surface, Cort moved behind a pine and squatted to get a lay of the land. He rubbed his pain-pounding left leg. In front of him, spreading from left to right, were three clusters of juniper trees, fresh green and taller than a man. Isolated mesquite plants dotted the sandstone surface

144

around the junipers. A group of pines and firs were at the far end, their trunks too thin to hide a man.

'I can outdraw you, Packet,' Utah Bill Slaughter said from the cluster of growth to the right.

'Mebbe. You should have dropped me when I reached the top.'

'I got a bead on you right now.'

'Then why wait?'

'Curiosity. How fast are you? I reckon Dougie is dead.'

'He is. Dugan and Blackwell and Red Jack Wheat too.'

'Then, you just got me.'

'I just got you.'

'Will you stand for a fast draw?'

Cort stood to stay behind the skinny pine. 'I recall you like an edge.'

'Ain't nobody up here except you and me. Where will the edge come from?'

'You'll find something.'

'We'll step out in the open with our holstered weapons, see who's quickest.'

Cort pushed the loop off the hammer of his Peacemaker. As he was about to step out, Slaughter fired from the Junipers. The bullet hit Cort in the upper muscle of his left arm. He spun to his left and grabbed a pine needle branch. Slaughter stepped out, firing again. He missed and thumbed the hammer back. Cort squatted again, the Colt in his hand, and shot Slaughter in the belly. Still down, Cort rolled as two bullets chewed sandstone. Cort fired twice quickly, both bullets going into Slaughter's head. Slaughter went to his knees. Cort rolled with his right leg under him and pushed to stand. The hammer was cocked again. Slaughter lay face down in a puddle, his Colt on the ground close to his head. Bubbles gurgled around his ear. Cort limped across and stood over him with his

Peacemaker aimed at the back of Slaughter's head, the hammer cocked.

Sunlight pushed to shine between clouds but a wind had come up to push dark cloud shadows slowly across the mesa surface. Cort watched Slaughter, blood dripping from the left sleeve of his slicker, an icy flow running through him, no vision, caring for nothing, the hammer on the Colt still cocked, ready to fire again.

The bubbles stopped.

TWENTY-SIX

The twice-a-week stagecoach waited in front of the Scarlet Hotel. Late morning sunshine brightened the town of Scarlet. Dode Lawson stood on the porch with his shotgun, the marshal badge pinned bright to his vest. He stroked his whisker chops and watched Inge hand her case to the shotgun rider who loaded it to the top of the coach. Dode had a chip torn out of his waist but it was bandaged tight by Doc O'Connor at the same time Cort had his arm wrapped. Both wounds were well on their way to healing by now. The marshal election went as expected. No competition. Somebody said Jesse Ryan ought to run, but like Cort, Jesse intended to be on his way along some trail.

Cort looked down at the pretty southern face of Rebecca Rogers. Jesse stood beside her. She had her hands folded in front of her, her big brown eyes locked on Cort's face.

'Jesse told me,' she said. 'You're going home to make things right.'

'I ain't got no home.'

She nodded. 'You think you'll be this way again?'

'No, ma'am.'

'You may have heard, Inge and I are to be partners. The stage will take us to the rail station in Santa Fe. We're headed for Yuma. We'll either buy a hotel there or have

147

one built.' She smiled at him. 'It appears I really am a rich woman. Mr Crutz paid me a handsome price for the silver mine, plus I get a percentage of all the silver that comes out.' She sighed. 'I would be quite a catch for some lucky man.'

'Yes'm.'

Jesse said, 'What happens after, Cort? What will you do after you settle this?'

Cort turned to Jesse. 'I got nothing planned after. You headed for Yuma too?'

Jesse looked down shaking his head. 'Not me, pard. I'm headed for Texas, down around the Red River Valley. I know people there. Might ride on down to Mexico.' He shrugged. 'Who knows? I might just amble on down toward Yuma eventually.'

Rebecca reached out and placed her palm on Cort's chest. She looked at his face with concern. 'Cort, Cort. If sometime down the road – I mean if you see your way clear – if you think it might work in your plans – if, if. . . .' She looked away, and after a sigh looked back. 'I'm just saying, if you ever find your way down around Yuma, you always got a free room at our hotel. It could be what you need will be waiting there.'

'*Ja,*' Inge said from the coach. 'A free room in our hotel. Cort, and you too, Jesse.'

Jesse cocked his head with a wink. 'Very tempting, little lady.'

Inge smiled at him.

Rebecca's arms went around Cort's neck. She pushed herself tight against him.

He had not held a woman since Amanda that morning so long ago in their bed. He had near forgot how good it felt. Rebecca seemed slightly taller, slimmer, but the curves were there against him and felt very good. Other feelings stirred within him that he thought he would never know again. She kissed his ear and stood back.

Cort bent and kissed her on the cheek. 'Don't be surprised if you see me ride into Yuma one of these fine old days,' he said.

TWENTY-SEVEN

Cort bypassed the Castro homestead because it was out of the way. He rode directly for the valley and the small spread of Ned and Martha Perry. He had no way of knowing if they had moved onto his property to rebuild or had brought his stock to theirs. He crossed the Rio Grande and rode northwest in the direction of Raton Pass, knowing he had to veer off thirty miles before he reached it. He carried beans, oats, beef jerky, smoked ham, and plenty of Arbuckle coffee and Bull Durham makings to use during the three-day journey. He carried three pint bottles of firewater in the saddlebags. Whiskey had wild grass to eat. He camped by streams for water.

When the land began to look familiar, he felt churning in his chest, the agitation of not knowing, not really, not for sure. He had killed four men. Two had nothing to say and died with silence on their lips. The other two, even knowing they were going to die, denied the acts, and carried that denial to their last breath.

Why?

His last night on the trail, he camped next to a creek, under cottonwoods and next to clumps of mesquite. As darkness fell, he leaned back on his saddle. He had used up the liniment Ada Castro gave him for his leg. The pain pricked him with a light ache so deep it seemed to come from the bone marrow, like somebody poked a nail into it. His left arm gave some bother too. Neither would slow him from what he had to learn and do. He would ride out from this valley with more knowledge, or with more killing than he had riding in.

Nobody had lived in the Perry cabin for more than two months or longer. Racoons and rats had moved in. Deer had eaten whatever crops grew. Bears had broken windows and destroyed whatever was left in cupboards and shelves. The stove was gone and the kitchen table and chairs, and the bed. Cort did not want to spend the night. He made one walk-through of the cabin and rode on.

At the place where he had found Amanda's body, he searched in a close circle. The grass that had flattened under her weight had grown back. No trace of blood remained. Cort widened the circle. When the man had struck her with a limb, and knowing the fight had gone out of her, he might have tossed the limb over his shoulder while he reached for her. Her dress had been torn off back by the stream where he left Billy-Boy. She only wore her thin cotton slip. Eight feet into the growth of firs, Cort found the limb, thick as a man's arm. A torn piece of the slip clung to splinters of it. He coughed to get the choke from his throat. Wiping his palms across his eyes he went back to the spot. He held the limb and squatted and tapped the limb on the spot. It had not been four men, not even two. It had been one man, a small man, a man who needed a weapon because the woman showed spunk and toughness and fought harder than he thought she would. He might have shot her, or pistol-whipped her as he did Billy-Boy, but that might have marked her. A few blows with the limb across her back and shoulders would have taken enough fight out of her for him to do his business. She would have still looked pretty, pretty and slim and docile enough for him to fulfill all his fantasy dreams. Afterward, she might have fought again and even shouted how slowly her husband would kill him or how her husband would give her the shotgun to do it herself. Hearing that, he pulled his pistol and beat the barrel across her face and head enough to kill her. He would not shoot her because of the noise. Other men were there stealing and burning. Good dumb luck for him, somebody to blame. As the men rode out, Cort rode in killing them one-by-one. Cort would blame them for Billy-Boy and Amanda and would continue to kill them until they were all dead and his revenge was complete. Then he would turn gunfighter again and go back to his old life until a faster-draw gunfighter shot him dead.

And Ned Perry would be free of blame.

Cort tossed the thick branch aside and mounted Whiskey. He rode away from the place, the clearing where his beloved Amanda had her life ended. He would never see it again. He rode across the stream where he had found the body of Billy-Boy and Amanda's torn green dress. He would never see that again, either. He continued to walk Whiskey until he saw the buildings.

A smaller cabin had been built next to the black silhouette Cort and Amanda constructed with their own hands. Chickens were in the yard with two pigs and the goat. As Cort rode into the yard, Martha opened the front door and stepped out with a carpet over her arm. She wore a plain brown dress and her black hair was in a bun. Her thin hawkish face held the red flush of housework labor. She looked up at him. She used her hand to brim her eyes against the glare and dropped the carpet. Her mouth opened wide.

'Cort? My God, Cort.'

Cort stayed in the saddle. 'Did he tell you, Martha? In his weakness, did he have a husband confessional one late drunken night, as husbands do? Did he tell you what he done? Did you know?'

'Know what? Cort, what in the world is wrong with you?'

Cort sat straight in the saddle, and shouted, 'Ned Perry, you son of a bitch, get on out here!'

From inside the cabin, Perry said, 'Get out of the way, Martha.'

Martha turned her back to Cort. 'What in the world is going on, Ned?'

Cort had his Colt in his hand. 'He pistol-whipped Billy-Boy to death. He raped and killed Amanda. He'll die for it.'

Martha turned back slowly as if she could not comprehend the words. She stared up at him, no color in her white face. 'Cort, that's . . . that's impossible.'

A shot came from the cabin that hit the well bucket. 'Martha, I told you to get out of the way. Move out from the door.'

She spun back around. 'Is it true, Ned? Did you do that? My God, I know you're weak, but I can't believe you'd do such a thing. Not even you.'

Perry fired again and Martha turned and stumbled out of the doorway clutching her chest. The carpet had been dropped inside the cabin doorway. Chickens clustered and flopped and hopped to get away. Martha stared at the ground. She hobbled two steps and sank to her knees and fell to her face. Blood pooled from under her. One of the pigs began to lap the blood.

Cort shot the pig. The gunshot sound ricocheted around the yard and off the far mountains.

Perry crashed through the back door and ran for the corral. Cort rode around, the Peacemaker still in his hand.

Perry needed no crutches but he limped to an unsaddled sorrel rein-tied to the corral gate. He yanked the reins loose and threw his leg over the bare back of the sorrel and pushed the horse through to open the gate. He rode away from Cort as fast as the sorrel could run toward range land used for cattle. Longhorns spread apart as if a wake peeled them while the sorrel speared through. Cort rode after him quickly closing the gap. Once clear of the cattle, Perry swung his boots out and in against the sides of the sorrel. He rode for the hills, slipping on the bare back. He twisted and fired a wild shot. Cort rode up behind and aimed for Perry's back. His shot missed as the sorrel stumbled with a scream, throwing Perry over his head. The sorrel's leg twisted double from a rabbit hole causing him to go down. Perry hit hard and tumbled forward, losing the Remington.

Immediately, Cort reined in already swinging his leg out of the saddle. He hit the ground on his good right leg. The sorrel lay on his side, his hoofs galloping through air. More screams of pain came from him. Cort shot the horse through the right ear, which silenced him.

On hands and knees, Perry scurried as fast as he could, still going for the hills, his fancy clothes muddied. Cort stepped to him and raised his leg and, with the heel of his boot on the spine, pushed down on Perry's back flattening him to the rocky mud. Perry turned and sat and rose to his knees. He stood brushing mud from his silk vest, small eyes fearful, lower lip quivering. Cort backhanded to rake his Colt across Perry's face. An open skin crease tore from jaw to nose and opened with a bleeding gash.

'No!' Perry cried. He bent slightly grabbing his face. 'You got it wrong, Cort,' Perry twisted back up and as he turned lunged at Cort with a bowie knife in his hand.

The blade sliced Cort's vest. Cort shot the hand holding

the knife. The Bowie fell to Perry's boot.

Perry gripped the shot hand and clutched it to his belly. He turned away, looking fearfully sideways at Cort. Fluid from his nose wet the aristocratic mustache. 'You got it wrong, Cort.'

Cort shot Perry's right shoulder.

Perry screamed. 'Don't. It wasn't fair. You seen Martha. You saw what I had. You had everything perfect. Perfect little ranch, perfect little family, perfect, beautiful devoted wife. And you, you nothing but a damned gunfighter. No reason for you to have it all. You didn't deserve it. You didn't deserve the perfect woman. She teased me. She was always strutting and sashaying around, bending and prancing, pouring coffee, making supper, moving in front of me teasing. She knew what she had. She knew what she was doing. She wanted *me* to do something.'

Cort shot Perry in the right knee.

'Aiee!' He fell to sit in the hard rocky dirt, his good hand holding the chewed knee. 'I carried it inside for too long. Two years I had the fantasy about how she teased and wanted me. I lay next to a cold woman who didn't even know how to show passion. And you, you had Amanda, flawless in every way. You had her there whenever you wanted her, you just had to reach out and your hands were filled with her. I couldn't wait. I had to, Cort, something drove me. Then, I couldn't tell nobody, certainly not Martha. I had to live with it. You got to understand, Cort. I'm real sorry about the boy, but he was trying to protect his mother. He hit me. When I tore at her dress, he threw rocks at me. Big rocks. I had to do what I did.'

Cort pulled the trigger but the Colt clicked empty.

Perry grimaced, panting in pain, unable to move or take advantage of the situation, bleeding and showing his pain. He fell back to his elbows. 'Martha once told me you were the only real man she knew. I believed her. That's why you'll stand tall now and be a man and forgive me what I done. That's what you'll do. You'll forgive me. We're kin. I'm your brother-in-law. You shot me up in punishment. But you punished me enough. You know that, don't you? You give me enough punishment and now you got to forgive me. Got to be a real man like Martha said and forgive me.'

The words hung in silence. Then the only sounds were Perry's ragged panting breath, and the leather squeak and metallic click of Cort emptying the Colt's cylinder and pulling cartridges from his gun belt. He pulled each one, turned it before his eyes, taking his time. He slid every cartridge on each side of his nose so they slipped one at a time easy into the Colt's cylinders.

Perry said, 'Can't you say something, Cort? Say you forgive me. I never meant to do it. It was them dreams, that image of her moving, the fantasy of her teasing me and wanting me and expecting me to do something. I know it was a fantasy now. I dreamed it all. I realized that when I had her there on the ground after I was done and only had the sweet memory.'

Cort fired again, the bullet squirting into Perry's chest.

Perry grunted with a frown and fell to his back. His eyes closed tight. 'Don't, Cort.'

Cort shot Perry in the forehead, putting an end to it.

A horse came up fast then slowed when next to Whiskey. Cort crouched and spun, the Colt hammer back, his finger on the trigger.

'I see you, Cort Packet,' Lorenzo Wolf Eater said.

TWENTY-EIGHT

With his lariat looped tight around Ned Perry's boots, Cort dragged the body behind Whiskey walking next to Lorenzo Wolf Eater's pinto.

'Your wife and boy,' Lorenzo said. 'It was not the cabin fire *hombres*, it was this one?'

'It was.'

'And his skinny unhappy wife?'

'He shot her dead.'

Lorenzo nodded. 'I have been looking after your one-eyed milk cow, Butter. She is well. She gives good milk.'

As they approached the cabin with Martha's body in the yard, Cort said, 'Go get some of your braves. Round up the cattle and all the stock and take them to the reservation. When the corn and vegetables come in have your women gather the harvest. There is hay in the barn you can use to feed the stock in the winter. There may be a mule in the barn with the horses. I will use the mule to pack provisions I get later. The horses are yours.'

'And you, Cort Packet?'

'I will not be here when you return.'

Lorenzo Wolf Eater rode his pinto ten steps away then turned back. 'Why? Why do this, Cort Packet? You can sell the cattle and the horses, and all the stock.'

Cort swung down from the saddle. 'I want your band to protect the graves on the hill.'

'Your wife and boy. They would be respected anyway. There is more.'

Cort looked up at the brave. 'I speak plain and slow to you, Lorenzo. I speak so you will understand. I am quarter Cherokee. I am also white. The white European invaders do not belong here, but here they are and here they will stay. They will take from all of you everything you have and leave you with nothing. And more will come. Invaders have always stomped onto lands and over the people there. It has been the way of men since time began. They will not be stopped. You cannot believe their empty words or the papers of written words. You cannot believe governments. Governments and invaders always lie. You and all your Indian brothers across this land will be trampled in the stampede of their numbers. There is nothing I can do about it. There is nothing you or your people can do about it. It will happen as certain as the turning of the earth.'

'We will fight,' Lorenzo said.

'You will fight and you will die. Your women and children will die. The children of your children will die. And white men will make those left of their children grow to be like them. You will go to their schools, live in their villages and towns and cities. White men will couple with your women until the blood is no longer pure. I come from that.'

'Was that bad for you?'

'No, for me it was good. My pa was white, my ma came from a Cherokee father and white mother. There was much love between them. It was good.' Cort looked off toward the mountain tops. 'I will never be this way again. What I loved is buried here and I have killed for my revenge. I cannot stay. I feel I must give away all I accumulated. I killed four innocent men, and that claws at me. It will take many years to forgive myself for that, if I ever do. Yes, they were guilty of stealing and fire but not for the reason I killed them.' He turned to look down at the bleeding body at his feet. 'He died for his deeds, for what he done. That was his punishment, his justice. My punishment for what I done is to go with only what I need. I want to leave your people better than when I came, better than when I lived here. Do you understand that, Lorenzo Wolf Eater?'

Lorenzo Wolf Eater also looked away, up toward the mountains. 'Maybe I will if what you say is true. I have always thought men can be reasonable. If it is not in their nature, they can be taught, whatever the color of their skin. You tell me there are men who will never be reasonable. If that is true, then your words of my people are true. I wish you a good journey, my friend, and that you find peace within yourself.' Lorenzo turned his pinto and rode out of the yard.

After Cort dragged the body of Ned Perry into the cabin, he clutched the wrists of Martha and dragged her inside to the opposite side of the room. He broke the three kerosene lamps against the walls and lit the cabin afire.

From the barn, he put reins on the grey mule and led her out and tied her to Whiskey's saddle horn. He had always thought mules were more intelligent than horses and made better pack animals. He mounted Whiskey and walked the chestnut to the hill and the graves, the mare mule obediently followed. At the graves, he dismounted and took the cane and pulled his hat.

'Billy-Boy, I know you still look after your ma wherever you are. She needs you now I ain't going to be around.'

He stepped to the grave beside the boy's. He choked when the words came. 'Ah, Amanda my precious girl, I am

159

so torn up inside. I got an ache in my chest big as a broken mirror. How can I amount to anything now, without you? Where will any gentleness come from? I know I got to move on but I wonder if I know how, you crowd my thinking so.' Tears flooded his vision. He dropped to his knees clutching the cane. 'My beautiful darling girl, I miss you so much. I ain't nothing without you. If I go back to bounty hunting, I'll be what I was when we met, more gunplay and shootouts. It don't sit right with me no more. I shot down four men who didn't need killing just yet. Not even God can forgive me for that. It will haunt me like the nightmare. But you know, girl? I don't have that nightmare no more. It went away. Mebbe what I done to those four men took over. I know I got to leave this place. I'm thinking I may head on down Yuma way. I've ridden that country and I know the territory. Mebbe I'll scout for the army out of Fort Yuma or one of them new forts they's always building. I may find something else there around Yuma that I ain't talking about to you jest yet.' He sniffled and sighed deep. 'You and the boy got a big chunk of my heart, girl, and that's a fact. It's a piece I'll never get back. I may never go as deep in feeling with nobody else. But, girl, I got to feel something for somebody, I jest got to. I can't keep holding this icy coldness and not caring inside me like I do now. I got to let myself go enough to let others in. I'm gonna try down there around Yuma. I love you, girl, you and my Billy-Boy son. I hope you like it wherever you are. But I'll be riding on now. I will think of you both often.'

Cort Packet used the cane to push to his feet. He put his hat back on and at the saddle shoved the cane next to his Winchester. He looked over his shoulder back to the graves and silently touched his index finger to the brim of his hat. He mounted Whiskey and with the mule in tow rode away.